The Scroll of Fate

The Scroll of Fate

KaCinderly Baker

ISBN: 0692070370
ISBN 13: 9780692070376
Library of Congress Control Number: 2018902510
KaCinderly Raconteur,Colorado Springs,CO

To
Dr. Michael J. Noble and Darla Olson
*I am grateful for Michael and Darla, who extend their goodwill and support
back into their community. They are stellar examples of people who generously
provide excellence in service to their profession and to humankind.
I dedicate this book—and my characters' steadfast fight to rescue the human race
from misfortune—to both of you.*

Thank you,
Michele Winter,
my dear friend whose opinions, feedback, and never-ending laughter I respect and take pleasure in.

One

HOSPITALS AND TOMBS

Their capture was no surprise. However, Eli had hoped for a more open environment when it happened. He had believed they would be taken while in the museum. Glancing around the enclosed passenger cabin, he realized how vulnerable they were. What if the driver had the same ability to paralyze captives that was used in the bunker? They could be rendered helpless in an instant, and they would have no chance to escape.

His thoughts were interrupted by Mariah, clutching his shirt as she wheezed a raspy, choking sound, and he saw her struggling for breath. The pale-blue outline around her lips meant this was a true emergency. Eli wondered if the driver was gassing them. Knowing he needed to act quickly, Eli turned his attention toward the driver and raised his voice. "Driver, take us to the nearest hospital now!" he ordered.

The driver, having quickly merged into the dense traffic, glanced in the rearview mirror, seeing an older man comforting a crying woman, and replied, "Welcome, Mr. and Mrs. Daniels. We can't go to the hospital now. I'm taking you to someone who is very anxious to meet you. If you need medical attention, a doctor might be called for you."

Eli closed his eyes for a moment while he gained his composure, and then he glanced at Mariah's pale face. He gently took Mariah's hand into his while placing her head tenderly on this shoulder. Pausing for a moment, Eli looked toward the driver. So as not be overheard, he softly whispered into her ear, "We are going to robe back to Denver, and I'll take you immediately to our doctor. Hang in there, sweetheart, and hold onto me because I'm going to recite the traveling prayer."

▲ ▲ ▲

The driver pushed a button to offer snacks and bottled water to his passengers, saying "First-class refreshments for my first-class passengers." Then, turning off the mic into the cabin, and confident he couldn't be heard, he spoke into his phone. "I have your two packages, and I'm bringing them to you."

Pleased with his progress, the driver glanced into the rearview mirror again and was shocked to see his passengers were not visible. They had disappeared. Quickly turning on the microphone to the cabin, he asked, "What are you guys doing back there?" He pulled over as swiftly as possible, and a cacophony of horns indicated the displeasure caused by his risky moves through the traffic.

The driver put on his emergency flashers and pulled off on the side of the road. Carefully he exited the cab, walked to the passenger's cabin windows, and peered into the back of the vehicle. He saw the bottled water, fruits, and cookies. However, there were no people.

The driver's posture stiffened. A split second later, he shuffled back a step or two, thinking that his passengers had somehow crawled into the trunk. A flush of adrenaline accompanied his steps to the back of the vehicle, where he popped the trunk open. His mouth fell agape as he viewed the empty trunk.

The driver was baffled and frightened. Both doors were locked, and there was no sign that anyone had ever been in the backseat. His body stiffened in fear.

He staggered slowly back to the driver's seat and sat down. His thinking was muddled because his mind was overcome by memories of the consequences of other people's failures. Beads of sweat formed on his upper lip and forehead, and he was overcome by an ever-growing sense of doom.

With a trembling hand, he grasped the phone and redialed the phone number he had called earlier. He spoke slowly into the phone. "The packages are lost." There was a pause, and then he cautiously added, "Yes, sir, I'll explain when I return." Ending the call, he realized that his voice had betrayed his fear at failure.

▲ ▲ ▲

After they landed back at the apartment in Denver, Eli rushed to the phone and called their family doctor. The receptionist realized the severity of Mariah's medical condition and instructed Eli to take Mariah directly to the hospital emergency room for assistance. The doctor would meet them there.

As he sped to the hospital, Eli reflected on the activities of the past several hours. He was not surprised that there were no special artifacts at the museum, but he was puzzled that no one had tried to abduct them there. This was obviously a trap and it seemed like it had failed.

I had thought they would capture us at the airport or at the museum, and when neither of these happened, I went to the first cab in line of the taxicabs, totally unsuspecting, and then we became trapped there. Of course they wouldn't try to capture us in public in front of everybody. This entire trip was foolish. Why didn't I just ask a colleague in New York to photograph the artifacts? Why did I expose both of us to this danger when we suspected the artifacts we need couldn't be there?

Still angry at himself for the foolish and hasty decision to go to New York, he pulled up to the hospital's emergency entrance.

▲ ▲ ▲

The hospital staff had quickly spirited Mariah off into one of their triage areas and pulled the curtain. Eli sat down nearby, and a woman in a surgical mask approached and asked him background questions about Mariah. He could hear himself giving answers: "She can't breathe…it started about an hour ago…no, this hasn't happened before…I'm not aware of any major allergies." And the questions continued as if Eli were in a dream. After the registration nurse had gotten all she needed from him, she returned to Mariah's bedside and shared Eli's answers with the staff assisting Mariah, and all Eli could see through breaks in the curtained area was a flurry of gowns and masks and paper booties.

The family physician arrived, nodded at Eli, and hurried into the triage room. Shortly afterward, the curtain was completely opened, and her gurney was pushed toward an elevator. The doctor then joined Eli, motioning for him to follow Mariah's gurney.

As they hurried down the hall, he began explaining her condition. "We're moving her to the ICU, where we can monitor her and keep her in quarantine until we know whether she is contagious. We can't do much more until the tests come back, which will probably take four to six hours. In the meantime, I need you to answer some questions for me. Has she been on any recent archeological expeditions, or has she been working on mummies or artifacts lately, especially anything from South America?"

Seeing the puzzled look on Eli's face, he continued. "Her symptoms are similar to those of valley fever. If it turns out to be that, it is curable if we have caught it early and begin treatment quickly."

Mariah was soon settled into her room, surrounded by a forest of poles that held IV bags; tubes and wires extended down and disappeared under the covers, and boxes with dials and lights and computer screens surrounded her. Each piece of equipment was set up and checked to ensure it was working properly. As the attendants began leaving, Eli asked if he could stay. They gave him a mask and gestured toward a comfortable-looking chair.

He sank into the chair and realized almost instantly how the effects of uncharacteristic activity and mounting stress had depleted his energy. As he rested, the sudden silence and absence of movement created a mental vacuum that was instantly filled with mounting remorse and depression. Tears ran down his cheeks as he contemplated a possible future without his beloved Mariah.

Remembering that the others needed to know their status, he pulled out his cell phone and texted, "Escaped trap. We are back in Denver." He would tell them about her health once he knew more.

He snoozed for several hours, drifting in and out of consciousness, unable to sleep due to worry and regret, as he kept wondering what he could have done differently.

The doctor aroused him from his stupor, and Eli listened alertly as the report was delivered. "The test results are back," the doctor began. "It does appear to be valley fever, as I suspected, and we caught it early. Mariah needs a week of bed rest and medication. We'll watch her tonight, and I will probably release her into your care in the morning. For now she needs a good night's rest with oxygen."

After the doctor departed, Eli set his phone on the bed beside Mariah, and then he laid his head down close to her hand to get some rest. He wanted to be as close as possible to her so that she would feel his presence and know he was there for her.

While Eli slept, people in gowns and masks were in and out of the room all night, checking charts and reading electronic displays, examining tubes and IV bags, and occasionally even checking the patient.

The next morning, the doctor returned, gave Mariah a quick check-up, and provided Eli information on the medications she would receive. He left and was soon followed by the release nurse, who gave hospital-exit instructions to both but concentrated on Eli since he was alert and Mariah appeared still somewhat groggy.

"We are releasing Mariah into your care, Mr. Daniels, and if she experiences any difficulty breathing, come back immediately. Follow the instructions on her medications. The main prescription is for an antifungal. Please don't hesitate to return if she is not getting better or her symptoms worsen. I circled your doctor's phone number in blue ink. Do you have any questions?"

Eli glanced at the paperwork and hastily read through the directions. "No," he responded. After the nurse departed, he checked his cell phone to see whether he had received any messages while he slept. Finding there were none, he put it back into his pocket and helped Mariah to the pharmacy.

After waiting a half hour for the prescription, Eli helped Mariah to the car. After assuring himself that she was comfortable, he closed her door and hurried to the driver's seat. He paused briefly before starting the engine. Seeing that she was nodding off, he leaned over and gently kissed her forehead and then began their drive back to the apartment.

Once there, Eli prepared the couch with extra pillows and a blanket. Making sure Mariah was comfortable, he shifted his attention to the kitchen and prepared a meal for them. He was surprised that a simple soup could taste so good, and then he realized he couldn't remember when he had last eaten.

Looking over at Mariah though, he could see she had barely tasted hers. She appeared listless and weak. Walking to the couch, he tenderly said, "I know you're tired, dear, but you must eat." Then, without forcing the issue, he gently helped spoon the hot, nourishing liquid into her mouth until it was gone.

Watching her while he washed the dishes, he couldn't help but notice that her labored breathing had improved, but she was struggling to keep her head up and her eyes open. "Are you OK?" he asked. "Can I do anything else?"

"I'm really tired," she said. "I want to go to bed."

He carried her to the bedroom and tucked her in. After pausing to watch her, he returned to the kitchen area. Still hungry, he threw together a sandwich and nibbled at it slowly, barely tasting it while his thoughts wandered. He stared out the large plate-glass window, watching the people below going about their routine lives, oblivious to the potential danger in their future that only a small team of strangers could prevent. With no pending activity to occupy his mind, he was flooded with worry and regret.

Why am I endangering Mariah and Sophia for them? Whether we succeed or fail, those people will never know what we did for them. Maybe we should quit now and leave this to Addison and Gabriel and Shamar. There isn't that much left to do: finding the shomer and a few more artifacts. Surely six people aren't any more effective than three?

Eli paced around the apartment, overwhelmed by emotion. Then he spotted an envelope on the desk that he hadn't noticed before. He picked it up and read the sticky note attached to it, which was in Sophia's writing. "I found this envelope addressed to you in the rabbi's glove compartment. Maybe it can help us."

Eli stared at the letter that he held tightly in his hands, knowing that if he opened it, he would do as it asked, and his loved ones would pay the consequences. So he stared at the letter, hating it for what it meant to his family and yet unable to set it down.

Not only did the rabbi's sudden, mysterious death feed his fear, but he doubted his ability to decipher the clues and complete the task levied on him by the rabbi.

Tiptoeing back to the bedroom, he checked in on Mariah and watched as she slept. He then returned to the couch, overcome with emotion. Then he made his decision and felt an unexpected release of tension as his eyes filled with tears.

After a few moments, he gently tore the envelope open and removed the letter that was probably the last information the rabbi had penned for him. Eli held on to the letter and humbly considered the obligation the rabbi had entrusted to him. He felt a rush of anxiety as he realized that the rabbi had formally placed the fate of the world in his hands, and he had knowingly accepted the responsibility.

▲ ▲ ▲

"Ouch!" Sophia exclaimed, after her feet landed on concrete. Surprised that this teleportation was different from the last one, she added, "We didn't fall asleep this time. I wonder why."

Still holding the embrace they had formed for traveling, Shamar answered, surprised, "You're right. I guess that only happens when we go back in time." He released her and glanced around, looking for something familiar. *Odd*, he thought, *there aren't many people around, and the few that are seem to be tourists, judging from their clothes and brochures.* With slight panic in his voice, Shamar said, "I'm not sure where we landed. This doesn't look like Alexandria. Could we have gone somewhere else?"

Sophia glanced around and thought they had landed near what appeared to be the ruins of an old amphitheater. She remembered a hand-drawn map that her parents had sketched of what they thought modern Alexandria would look like. Anxiously she retrieved the map from her backpack.

Shamar joined her, and they pivoted in a full circle, comparing the map to the landscape, looking for something familiar. Nothing appeared right. And then, to their delight, they saw it at the same time: Pompey's Pillar.

"We didn't land at the base of the pillar this time," Shamar observed. "Whatever is serving as our beacon must have moved." After a pause he added, "I'll tell the others we arrived." He texted the others: "Arrived in Alexandria. Both safe."

Relieved that she finally realized where they were, Sophia excitedly gave Shamar a hug and a peck on the cheek, and then, grabbing his hand, she headed toward the pillar. As they made their way there, they had to step around bits of ruins, both astonished at what the ravages of time had done to the big monument since they had last seen it sixteen centuries earlier.

Surveying the rubble that surrounded her, Sophia remarked, "Did you know that the destruction of the library and this surrounding area has been documented at least nine times? It has been damaged by two earthquakes and a tsunami, fires, mob violence, and most recently Israeli bombs, in the last century."

Now able to compare her mother's map with a known landmark and observing the locations of the remaining lion statues relative to the pillar, she could make an educated guess regarding the location of the sister library. She grabbed Shamar's sleeve and pulled it, saying, "Let's go this way. I'm certain that I know where we are."

They proceeded a few hundred yards with Sophia frequently glancing back at the pillar and lions to check her bearings, and then they had to stop. The way forward was blocked by a makeshift chain link fence that surrounded all access to the ruins of the sister library. She let out a small whimper as she read the signs posted on the fence.

"What does it say?" asked Shamar.

"This one says that a government historical group is doing reconstruction of this area, which they think was once a secret entrance to the sister library.

Other signs state that people must keep out due to the dangers of unmarked holes and tripping hazards and other dangers from old tunnels."

"Now I know why there are so few people around," Shamar said. "No one can see anything because it's all closed for construction."

Sophia quietly studied the layout.

"What are you thinking?" Shamar asked as he watched her expression change from disappointment to determination.

With a sigh, Sophia put her arm around his waist and said, "We haven't come this far to let a little restoration work stop us. I'm wondering how we might use this to our advantage. As you can see, someone has already done some of our digging for us. I hope they haven't destroyed the old tunnel that we have to find."

Shamar smiled and took her hand, and said, "I'm hungry. Let's go get something to eat and talk about our plans for this evening. After dinner and with the cover of darkness, we'll climb over the fence and begin our investigation."

Departing the area, they observed that they were surrounded by buildings with lots of windows and some doorways but few signs, and most of the signs they could see were not in English.

"I hope you can figure out which one of these places has food," Shamar said.

"Not a problem," Sophia answered. "Let's follow our noses." She smiled confidently.

Inviting smells came from a doorway, and she said, "Let's try this place." They entered through the door and were shown to a table by an amiable server, whom they discovered did not know English. After studying the menu for a while, Sophia asked in Arabic for recommendations. He answered, and after a brief discussion, he was gone, eventually returning with two plates of food.

"What did you order?" Shamar asked.

Sophia was embarrassed. "Unfortunately I didn't pay attention in language class when we learned foods. I told the waiter to bring us foods that he thought Europeans would like. So the short answer is, I don't know."

After making a great effort with the alien tastes and playing a game of guessing what some of the entrees were, they began discussing their plans.

Their first consideration was how they would go about finding the tunnel and supplies they would need.

They opened their backpacks to see what Addison had provided for them. Besides local currency, they found flashlights, batteries, and trail mix. Shamar found a modern street map of Alexandria.

The waiter returned, asked how the supper was, and had a short discussion with Sophia. He returned a short time later with two small cups of coffee. It tasted good, but it was strong and gritty.

"It's almost time," Shamar said. "We need to stay focused. Our objectives are to find the tunnel, locate and decipher the slabs that your father found, and if possible learn the purpose of those three doors." They paid the bill, thanked the proprietor, and headed back to the ruins, walking hand in hand.

"I never really appreciated how important it was to have Theon guide me through the cultural variances," Shamar said. "We can't order food, we don't know where to sleep, and we don't even know how to find a public bathroom."

"You should have asked at the restaurant," Sophia said. Now you're out of luck. Speaking of sleep though, if we work all night, we will need a private place to rest in the morning."

"If it's still available, we could try the Temple of Canopus," Shamar said.

"The catacombs?" she asked incredulously.

"Why not?" he answered, with a grin.

"Because it's eerie and it stinks!" she replied.

They arrived at the area under construction. While they waited for more darkness and privacy, Sophia checked her phone for messages and updates. She read her father's text—"They have us"—and a tear ran down her cheek.

Seeing her distress, Shamar put his arm around her and looked at her phone to see what upset her. He was shocked when he read her father's message; however, he noticed that there was a second message. "Let's see what the second message says." He pulled it up. "Look. They escaped and are safe in Denver."

Shamar could see that doing nothing while they waited for a chance to sneak into the site unseen was not good for Sophia. "Your parents will be fine. Your dad isn't going to let anything or anyone hurt your mother. They are probably planning right now to come join us, and we will need to have answers. Gabriel and Addison will also be joining us as well."

As a soft evening breeze moved stealthily across Shamar's face, he felt uneasy, as if they were being watched. Shamar slowly looked around. Soon his eyes caught the sight of a single person looking their way. "Don't look, but someone is watching us. It might only be a security guard on his rounds, but I am not sure."

Tenderly, Shamar embraced Sophia and kissed her. She responded favorably, and he slowly released her. "Thank you," he whispered. "I think our watcher now believes that we are just tourists out enjoying this lovely evening."

"He's right," Sophia softly responded. "I am enjoying the evening."

Shamar winked as he squeezed her hand, and Sophia blushed.

They walked aimlessly, pretending to be lovers out for a stroll, until they were confident that everyone was gone. Shamar said, "It's time," and he began climbing the fence. Since it was only a temporary, makeshift fence, it leaned toward him, and he had to get down.

"This won't work. We have to find a break in the fence. They won't like it if I pull it down." They found a spot where two fence segments joined, and they were able to squeeze through the joints and walk over to the excavation.

Sophia gasped in surprise. What had appeared to be a long, wide trench was a meticulously terraced hole that reminded her of a strip-mining project, going down into the earth about fifteen or more feet, with the deepest part adjacent to the ruin that was at the Serapeum Temple. This did not seem like a restoration project to her or Shamar.

Shamar saw a ladder leading down into the pit. He held the ladder as Sophia eased her way down to begin their exploration. Looking up, she motioned for Shamar to descend.

Taking in the surrounding area, they could see that this trench extended the length of the foundation of this ancient ruin with a second tunnel ahead and to the left, which appeared to open up into the foundation. Using their lights, they examined the tunnel or cave that had been excavated, and together they entered the opening of the foundation.

"I wonder if this is the secret tunnel my mother and father were in?" Sophia said. "It does appear to go back toward Pompey's Pillar, as sketched on Mother's map."

"They excavated this section thoroughly," Shamar remarked, noticing that they were walking on a section of stone tiles that had been placed to make a floor. As they continued down the dark passage, they studied the floor, walls, and ceiling for any signs that might indicate whether this was the tunnel that Mariah had described to them.

The air was damp and smelled moldy. As they passed small trash bins, Shamar checked the contents, hoping for clues within the trash. After checking a few, he concluded, "There's nothing here but trash, dirt, and rocks. Most likely," he added, "any artifacts they found have been catalogued and removed."

Further down the passageway, they noticed a change in the floor coloration, which they attributed to dirt that had fallen from the ceiling. Looking up they became aware that dirt had indeed fallen, exposing an odd-shaped opening into a higher level.

Shamar grabbed a nearby refuse container and stood on it, allowing him to peer into the hole. Even with a flashlight, he couldn't see anything. "We'll come back to this later if this tunnel goes nowhere," he said.

Looking at Mariah's map, Sophia speculated that this hole might be near the old secret entrance to the tunnel, and that it could be because of this hole that modern archeologists had discovered the tunnel. However, she remained doubtful because this area seemed more like a forgotten dark, dank cellar.

Her thoughts changed quickly though, when their flashlights illuminated faint traces of markings on the wall that resembled some descriptions of the wall markings from her mother's map. "I believe we're close," she said. "And I think the secret room should be just ahead of us."

Then, several steps further on, they came upon a small archway that may have once been a door, and looking down at the map, they believed they were very close to where a door was indicated. This opening widened a little and led them into a room about the size of a small bedroom.

A stifled squeal of excitement escaped from Sophie's mouth. "We found it!" she exclaimed. "This has to be the same room that my parents found when they were here. I feel that we are on the right track." Newly energized, she twirled in a circle.

Shamar grinned, happy to see her smiling again and bubbling over with enthusiasm and confidence. They waved their flashlights around, looking for more indications that this was the place they were seeking. If there had been shelves, tables, or scrolls, they had all been removed.

"This room is a dead end," Shamar said. The map shows a door on that wall over there." He pointed with his flashlight. They both went to the wall to see if they could find an opening. Remembering what Quintus said about this area, Shamar was successful in finding what he needed to open the way to a hidden passage.

They both felt the cool air pass over them quickly as they entered this room. Shamar looked at Sophia and said, "Don't look down. Quintus said the depth on either side of this bridge is unknown. Just stay focused on crossing the bridge and going through the tunnel to the doors and slabs."

Together they crossed the bridge and followed the narrow tunnel. The only sound was the soft crunch of their shoes on the tunnel's small stones on the floor. Sophia felt the atmosphere to be unpleasant, and she didn't understand why. She whispered, "Shamar, I'm scared. This is a creepy tunnel. It's cold, small, reeks of an odor I can't identify, and definitely doesn't feel right."

Shamar's response was swift. He stopped, turned to face her, and spoke in a firm, soft voice. "I agree. And we need to be quick with our investigation because I don't feel comfortable here either." Looking into Sophia's face, Shamar leaned in toward her, gave her a gentle kiss, and taking her hand into his, resumed leading their way down the tunnel.

A short time passed, and they came upon the opening each had heard others describe. It was the end of the tunnel, actually a *T* intersection in which there were three slabs on the floor and what appeared to be three doors set into the wall just above the slab below. Each end door was adjacent to the tunnel in its own small alcove, separate but still a part of the tunnel.

Sophia immediately began examining the slabs, and Shamar explored the walls that looked like the doors Quintus had said he didn't have time to investigate. He remembered that Quintus had thought that something was hidden behind the doors. Both felt a soft tremble as the ground beneath their feet shook and dust flickered from above them, settling down all around them.

"Did you feel that?" asked Sophia.

"Yes," replied Shamar. "I wonder if the workers have returned to the site. They must have come in a big truck."

There was complete silence, and each looked at the other for a moment, waiting to see if anything else would happen.

Sophia crouched down between two of the slabs on the floor. She opened her backpack and took out a small paint brush. Next she began brushing off the slabs to read the inscriptions. Slowly she wrote down what she had uncovered.

Shamar thought he heard something, so he turned quickly and touched Sophia on the shoulder. When she looked up, he had his finger across his lips, letting her know to be silent. She listened too as she came up and stood beside Shamar. Soon she also heard the slow and methodical movement of someone walking down the tunnel toward where they were.

The sound of the footsteps stopped, and they both heard the murmur of a person followed by another low voice. They both heard someone verbalize in a commanding voice, "We are to take them alive." Next they heard the footsteps resume, and this time they could distinguish footsteps of more than one person walking toward where they were, and at a faster pace.

Sophia grabbed her items and shoved them into her backpack; she quickly zipped it shut, placed it over her shoulders, and then immediately positioned herself in Shamar's arms. Shamar, without hesitation, embraced her and said the prayer, and both were transported.

Two

The Phantom Reveals His Plan

Vincent awoke abruptly with the feeling that someone was in his room. That was probably related to his dream. He couldn't remember the specifics, but he knew he had been really hot, and his throat burned. Plus he had experienced an overwhelming feeling of despair. Needing a glass of water for his parched throat, he rolled to get out of bed but paused when he saw a piece of paper on the nightstand. It was slightly charred and still glowing at the edges as if it had been on fire. *Am I still dreaming?* He didn't think so.

There was a note. He reached for it and read its contents. The words were not written in pen or pencil but were charred into the paper as though formed with a glowing hot pen. The note read, "I am waiting for you in the dining room." The note was not signed, but it didn't need to be. Vincent became nauseous, as he always did when he had to meet the note's author. He rose and donned a robe and slippers. The water would have to wait, as he knew he was expected to respond immediately.

Fully awake now from a rapidly increasing heartbeat and a deep sense of dread, he shuffled into the dining room, where he saw the man he only knew as the phantom sitting at the table. This time he appeared as a middle-aged man. Although he manifested himself differently each time they met, Vincent always knew who he was.

Ever since that first meeting, his life had changed for the better, and he had everything he wanted—money, power, and women—and all he had to do was an occasional job. The phantom had originally told Vincent that he was Lucifer's emissary to the world, but Vincent didn't believe him. He thought he was a delusional old man. But as time passed, Vincent had come to wonder whether this incredulous claim could be true.

"Welcome, sir," Vincent managed to whisper through his parched lips. As their eyes met, he noticed the phantom's hands were clasped tightly and his knuckles were white.

The phantom stood and walked over to him. After studying him for a few moments, he said, "I am losing confidence in you, Vincent. It seems to me that you don't fully understand the significance of this project. If you did, we wouldn't be having this conversation about your continual problems."

Vincent could feel the adrenaline rushing through his system, preparing his body for its natural fight-or-flight response. Unfortunately, neither option could help him now.

"I know how important this is," Vincent answered. "That is why we are working so hard to get everything done." He tried to swallow, but his dry throat just burned more. Then he continued, "And I think my team is doing pretty well. I have everyone you asked me to watch under surveillance, and when the watchman shows up, we will know immediately and dispose of him."

The temperature in the room increased uncomfortably as the phantom said, "Don't lie to me. If they are under surveillance, tell me where they are right now."

Vincent had known that his words were a mistake as soon as he had uttered them. He clarified his statement by explaining, "What I meant was, Eli and Mariah are in New York. As for the rest, we will soon have bugs on every phone Eli might call and cameras on every place he and Mariah might go. We will have them very soon."

The phantom seemed to grow in stature as he levitated off the ground slightly and looked down on Vincent, and the room became even warmer. The phantom said, "You have overestimated your abilities and those of your team, as shown by the number of gross errors that now endanger this mission. The damage can't be undone, but you have one last chance to recover and regain control.

"Let me remind you of the mistakes. Senka's henchmen killed the rabbi before we had all his information and, *very* importantly, specific artifacts. Had he been allowed to live a little longer, we would have had everything we need by now.

"Then, the attempt to recover artifacts from Edward's secret bunker failed, immediately followed by Senka detaining and imprisoning a simple, clueless girl, who successfully escaped from a team of guards and dogs then evaded and continues to evade our surveillance.

"After that, Senka's little trick to get the police to find our desired targets has now attracted law enforcement attention. Does any of what I have described sound like you have everything under control?"

There was no answer.

After suspending his questioning for a moment, the phantom continued. "We are trying to carry out a covert operation to obtain the people and things that could stop us—stop us!—and therefore jeopardize the mission. Since the people who can stop us now know that we are looking for them and are more aware of our desires, our job has become much harder. That is why I am here. Because on your watch, your team has lost track of everyone we need to find, they have not gathered a single item that is critical for us to have, and they have forgotten what our goal is."

The phantom retreated a few steps back and then pivoted, irritably staring at Vincent for an answer.

"Yes," Vincent responded timidly. "You're right that the people we hired were not the best. But my team is working harder to recover from our failures."

The phantom turned away from Vincent and began pacing within the dining room. After a long pause, he continued. "So you believe that this operation has been reset and your problems have been resolved. I hope so. You realize, of course, that the only reason you are not a pile of ash right now is because I don't have time to train your replacement."

Vincent's face paled, and he said nothing. The phantom drank in the new surge of fear that emanated from Vincent.

With a condescending smile on his face, the phantom spoke up, asking, "By the way, what became of Sago?"

Continuing, he said, "Last I heard, Vincent, Senka was upset at him and blamed him for her failures. However, I don't remember anyone telling me where his body is."

There was a temporary halt as the phantom considered how to resume his scolding. "I don't know why you put her over him," he said. "You would have been wise to leave Sago in charge. Before you put her in charge, Sago was a master of stealth and attention to detail. I liked his work, and I never worried about results. He did have one flaw though. Although he liked money and power, he had a weakness for certain individual humans. In our business, you must accept that we sometimes must sacrifice one or two for the good of the mission. You can't let feelings get in the way.

"And since I brought her up," he said, "what is Senka up to? I must agree that she has the right attitude, but she lacks management skills. I can't afford to have someone on staff that spends an entire career fixing her own mistakes. You should make note of that last statement, Vincent."

Continuing his cold stare and adding a sinister smile, he added, "She is very attractive. Perhaps she would be more useful in my office, where she can take over other duties. Some of the pretties who work for me are becoming tiresome. I think Senka will present a perfect challenge for me."

Vincent was horrified. He had plans of his own for Senka, and he also thought she had great potential for recruiting people and that together they would make the perfect team. With a slight quaver in his voice, he protested, "Perhaps we could give her another chance. Some of the disasters under her were not entirely her fault."

Another mistake! Vincent recalled being warned about questioning any decisions the phantom made. The temperature in the room again rose, and even skin that was protected by clothing was beginning to burn.

Eventually the phantom began to cool off, and he explained, "Let me remind you, we have worked for thousands of years to arrive at this moment.

"We now have our chance, this one opportunity to seize the stone. Aaron's stone and the accompanying traveling gems have resurfaced after disappearing with the destruction and looting of Solomon's Temple. The essence that empowers those gems that was sealed into special crystal flasks centuries ago has emerged, and we know this because that essence has reached us. All this, coincidentally, at the same time that our master will have his only opportunity to return to earth to conquer its inhabitants.

"Lucifer, my master, loves humans and realizes that humans need conflict to grow stronger and succeed. War, pestilence, and famine are tools to fell the weak, weed out the pathetic, and starve the wretched, leaving only the strong.

"With this stone, The Thirteenth Stone of Aaron, in our possession, we can expand our influence and control of world leaders. We can cause wars and conflict whenever we choose. We will make humanity better and more deserving of survival and Lucifer's love. With this stone we will make civilization better.

"All that is stopping us is one man in a continuous line of Jews who have effectively escaped centuries of persecution, and a handful of artifacts that should have been destroyed centuries ago.

"Let me reemphasize, we have only one chance. History is in the making. If you blow this, humankind's weakness and our inability to take care of them for the rest of eternity will be on you." He paused for effect. "You, Vincent, a single human being, will be responsible for the demise of the entire human race."

When he finished, he was gone. He didn't fade away or walk out the door or disappear in a puff of smoke. He was just not there.

Vincent, suddenly alone with himself, wondered briefly if this was a dream. But he knew it was not. *Billions of people miserable for eternity just because of me,* he thought. *I think I would be better off if he had turned me into ashes.*

He looked at himself in the mirror and saw what most people could not because he had been given the talent to influence people to see him as he wanted them to. His face, if seen without paranormal influence, displayed an ugly scar from above his left eyebrow to the tip of his nose. A milky eyeball in the middle was a reminder of the cost of minor failure. He also saw what appeared to be sunburn on all his exposed skin, including his arms and face. On closer inspection, he noticed small blisters on his arms, resulting from the heat radiated from the phantom.

Senka popped into his mind. He would miss her. He had chosen her because of her devious disposition and total absence of remorse. It was unfortunate that she couldn't manage a project. People as devoid of conscience as she was were rare.

He didn't return to bed, knowing there would be no sleeping, so he spread out his files across his desk to devise a plan.

First he had to analyze the enemy. His first enemy was Eli, presumably the designated successor to Rabbi Katz. He and his wife, Mariah, probably knew the big picture and if captured could identify where everything and everyone of importance was. Then there was Addison, the butler to a dead archeologist, who had been secretly storing artifacts as they turned up. Sophia, daughter to Eli and Mariah, had seemed to know nothing, but after her capture she had gone to the rabbi's home to steal his car. What does she really know about the rabbi? Then there was Shamar, Sophia's friend, who had no history involving the artifacts but seemed to show leadership and loyalty and had fought against Sago in the bunker confrontation. Gabriel clearly was a hired goon, only there to protect everyone. And last, there had been an oddly dressed stranger in the bunker among this group. *Who is he? I have no file on him.*

All right, who is the weak link? If I can neutralize Sophia and her parents, then Shamar will be helpless. She must be injured or killed. Injury might be preferable, since killing might invoke vengeance. And capturing Addison would be useful since an enterprising inquisitor could learn everything about the artifacts from the old Edward expedition.

But we'll take whoever we can get. I need a status update.

He established a telephone conference with the chiefs of all the teams. "No change from before" was the message from everyone. It seemed that all their subjects except for Eli and Mariah had disappeared from the earth.

"OK," he said. "Keep it up. They can't hide forever. Make sure we have everything covered. Where they work, school, doctors, friends, restaurants, grocery stores. Go through their trash. If you can find old credit-card receipts or bills, find out where they spend money, and watch those places."

After the call terminated, the phone rang again. It was Senka! He listened to her but couldn't overcome his fear that this might be a trap. She had a new idea to provide an anonymous tip that Addison's house had stolen contraband from Edward's old archeological expedition that had involved Eli and Mariah.

More bad ideas! he thought. Vincent found it difficult to say anything. His ability to speak was restricted by his fear of what the phantom would do to him. Paralyzed by his knowledge of the phantom's plan for her and what he knew about the phantom's opinion on attempting to trick law enforcement into helping, he remained silent. He thought, *And if I help her, my fate will be worse than hers.*

"Are you still there?" she asked.

"Yes," he said, "I'm still here and still thinking of your idea." *Why hasn't the phantom contacted her yet?* His nausea returned. Slowly and with a somewhat slurred voice, he asked her, "What are your other ideas?"

He wanted to tell her what had just transpired, but he dared not.

What he didn't say to her spoke volumes. "Tell me what's going on," she pleaded.

"I can't help you" escaped from his mouth before he could stop it, and he quickly hung up, not wanting to have any further contact with her.

The phone rang again. His elite team manager in New York had news for him. *Thank goodness it is not Senka.* But this was bad news. "Senka's package escaped from the cab we hired…"

"What do you mean, 'escaped'? How could you let an old man and old woman flee from a locked cab?"

"It's a puzzle to us" was the answer. "They literally disappeared. There's no trace of them, and all the doors are still locked. But it gets stranger," the man said. "About an hour later the Denver office called me. Eli and Mariah appeared in a hospital in Denver. It seems that Mrs. Daniels is sick. I don't know how they got there, but we got a break.

"Our operative managed to bug Eli's phone while they were asleep at the hospital, and we can now monitor all their phone traffic. It has already paid off, as we received a text from Shamar reporting that he and Sophia arrived safely in Alexandria. It didn't say which Alexandria though. I think Virginia is more likely than Louisiana."

Vincent knew which Alexandria it was. *So, they have learned how to use the robes and their traveling gems for certain. That is the only way they could go to Denver in less than an hour and to Egypt without us seeing them in the airport. And now I understand how they got out of the bunker.*

The team manager asked for his new instructions.

Drawing in slow, steady breaths before proceeding, Vincent coldly asked, "Has Senka been informed? And if so when, and what was her response?"

"A message was left on her cell" was the answer. "And we have received no response so far."

Vincent said, "You and your men have done a magnificent job. Keep me informed immediately when anything happens. Thanks again." He disconnected the call.

How many of them have mastered travel with the robes, and how much do they know about their gems' capabilities? Do they know about the watchman, and have they found him yet? I have to stop them. Maybe the Daniels will lead me to the watchman's exact location through cell phone usage.

He called his pilot and secretary. "We are leaving for Alexandria, Egypt, as soon as we can. And get me as many security people as possible for this trip."

▲ ▲ ▲

Senka was worried. She had to have some type of success, and soon. Following her instinct she called INTERPOL and provided them a tip about possible criminal activity by Addison and the now-deceased Edward regarding the theft of Egyptian artifacts from Edward's archeological expedition several years earlier. She suggested that the house maintained by Addison for Edward's son, Patrick, was full of concealed contraband.

Feeling intense heat on her back as she hung up, she spun around, and there before her was the phantom.

▲ ▲ ▲

Addison and Gabriel robed into Ancient Alexandria, landing with Gabriel's arms tightly wrapped around Addison.

Gabriel was awakened suddenly by the strong smell of alcohol and a firm hand shaking his shoulder. Instinctively he pushed back and a startled voice responded, "hey man I'm just trying to help you. I don't want to fight. When they find drunks sleeping on the street they stone them". As his head cleared Gabriel realized the man was just trying to help. "Thanks", Gabriel said, as he sat up and tried to awaken Addison.

Gabriel, more concerned about safety and security, looked around for a friendly face as people passed by. None of Quintus's or Avitus's men were around. The few people who were close to them glanced at them suspiciously but didn't give them any trouble.

After they began walking in the direction of the library, they recognized a few of Avitus's men and approached them quickly. "Hey, friends," Addison called out. "We need to find Avitus, Quintus, and Theon. Can you please help us?"

Being familiar with the two guests and understanding their urgency, they promptly escorted them to the Great Library. As they passed through the streets, they were subject to stares as people stopped what they were doing to watch them. Some displayed frightened expressions and hurried away from them. It was clear that all of them had heard about the incidents they had been involved in, and some of them might have been among the crowds that had tried to fight with them when rioters had been killed.

Addison could tell already that their planned trip to search for the flask would be a great deal harder and more dangerous than their other visits. The local people were clearly hostile, and he and Gabriel would need protection from them just as much as from bands of thieves.

After the short, tense walk to the library, they knocked on Theon's door, listening for any sounds inside. The door opened and they saw Theon's eyes peering through the narrow opening to see who was calling.

"Please enter quickly," Theon said. As they did he looked beyond them to see whether anyone had seen them enter and immediately closed the door behind them.

After initial greetings, Addison excitedly explained why they had returned. "We have to go to Heracleion and find a glassmaker, one who makes double-walled flasks and can use sand between the walls to make a design. We must have such a flask with a phoenix design."

After Theon had impatiently listened to the request, he hurried back to the door and locked it.

Both men found his behavior unnerving. After locking the door, Theon paused to listen to the sounds outside, and then the three men gathered around the table. He shushed Addison, and said, "I know your trip here is necessary, but each time you visit, the danger increases to the library and to everyone who has associated themselves with you. The situation has gotten worse since your last visit."

Theon clasped his hands together and placed them on the table and was deep in thought.

After a long pause, when Gabriel was about to speak, Theon finally began. "As I stated, things have changed for the worse in the short time you were gone. The streets are more dangerous by day and by night, and the citizens of Alexandria are taking refuge in their own homes, leaving only when they must, for shopping or to work. I know Quintus can't spare any soldiers due to the unrest, and I don't know whether Avitus can escort you to Heracleion or anywhere else."

Addison slumped in his chair and pulled his glasses down his nose. "We must go to Heracleion. We know it is dangerous, but we don't have a phoenix flask, and we believe that this is our only chance to get one. We'll go alone if we must, but we would rather have help. I have to speak to Avitus to see whether he can help."

Standing, Addison pulled a package from his pocket and placed a pouch on the desk in front of Theon and continued. "I have brought what I believe is a fair payment for whoever can help. We just need to speak with the glass-maker and learn whether he has the flask we need or if he can make one for us. That is all we plan to do."

Theon looked into the pouch and saw a small pile of gold and silver bullion. "It doesn't matter how much gold or silver you brought," he quickly said. "The soldiers are busy protecting the citizens of the city, and they are worried about their families due to the dangerous attitudes of certain Alexandria citizens, many of whom can unleash death or serious injuries upon the soldiers and their families. I doubt that any will be available."

"Can we ask anyway, in case they can free up just one or two?" Gabriel asked. "I'm sorry about your trouble, but we will have worse trouble in our time if we don't succeed. We wouldn't have asked if this weren't crucial."

Theon answered, "I'm certain that Avitus and Quintus will be here as soon as they know you have come back. They both respect each of you—especially you, Gabriel, for the help you gave them when you were here before."

Theon changed the subject. "I must share another matter with you both, especially you, Gabriel. When I first found the secret room, even before I knew Shamar, I read a unique scroll that evaporated into a fine mist when I finished reading it. It was at that moment that I realized I was the only person who could ever possess its knowledge.

"This scroll alerted me to the coming of Shamar and described his robe and explained how helping this person would be crucial to the future of humankind. When the scroll evaporated, I absorbed all its information, to include a translation of mysterious chanting that haunted me from within the library. It also explained that Shamar had to be supported and defended at all costs.

"Then an apparition appeared to me, and this individual seemed real. He was none other than Aaron, the brother of Moses."

Addison was shocked, and said, "Aaron? Why didn't you share this with us before, and why are you telling us now?"

Gabriel, feeling he was being blessed by hearing a witness to a divine vision, crossed himself and anxiously hung on to every word. He whispered, "Bless you, Theon, and bless you."

"Why?" Theon repeated, addressing his answer to Addison. "Because I understand that I have completed all my responsibilities for this mission. It is now up to Shamar and his colleagues in the future to finish the job. It is at this time, now, right now, that I know I must share the remainder of the information to the people who must carry on."

Still looking at Addison, he continued. "I knew you would be back; I just didn't know when." Turning to Gabriel he said, "Your important battle will take place in your time, Gabriel. The rabbi Katz had traveled back and forth between times, first to gather knowledge and missing items and later to store the items that he deemed essential to this mission, for protection and so that the relics were out of reach of his modern enemies. When the battle comes, it will be vital for all of you to protect Shamar and the other important individual, who will seal the door before it allows evil to come through and enslave humankind. Your job, Gabriel will be to make sure that nothing interferes with the two people who are performing the ceremony. Others will have key jobs as well. The wearer of the phoenix robe must direct where each person stands, as defined by the scrolls that you recover. Others in the battle, probably Eli and Mariah, will provide the intellect and research."

Gabriel, with confusion in his voice said, "I don't understand. I am just a bystander who was asked to tag along and help. Why do you think I have an important part in this mission?"

Theon answered, "I was given a vision of what will happen. I have seen that the Great Deceiver will plant ideas to drive your group apart, and some of you, sadly, will be fighting among yourselves more than you will be fighting an enemy. Everyone must pay attention to what is happening, and you, Gabriel, with your heightened sense of awareness, must be ready to intervene if it appears one of you could be falling for deception, and you must prevent that person or persons from spoiling the ceremony.

"You, Addison," he said, "must be prepared to help as well. You might have to restrain someone close to you personally. It will be difficult for Eli, especially, since the dearest objects in his life, his wife and daughter, are his weaknesses, and these weaknesses can be used to manipulate him.

"And, Addison, there are great dangers ahead. Evil believes that you have knowledge that they seek, and they will try and extract it from you. Trust no one except for Shamar and Gabriel and the other three in your group. Trust no one else. There is one exception. Someone may approach you to help save you at his own peril. If that happens, accept his sacrifice, and move on.

"You are correct that you need a phoenix flask, but I am troubled about the trip you must make to secure it. And, it is not just your lives that are at risk. The essence in the flasks will be threatened as well. If evil can destroy the essence, your chances of success will be diminished."

Looking down at his table and again folding his hands together, Theon sat in silence.

Three

THE DOUBLE-GLAZED PHOENIX FLASK

The mood was somber as Theon prepared hot water for tea while they waited for the arrival of Quintus and Avitus. All three men realized that this was likely to be their last time together. Theon was certain that his duties were complete in this venture, and the increasing danger in the streets of Alexandria made each successive trip here by Shamar, Gabriel, Addison, Eli, or Mariah more hazardous for him.

A sharp rap on the door broke the silence, and Theon unlocked it to let in Quintus and Avitus. The men quickly embraced and then settled down into discussions of the latest developments in both worlds.

Gabriel pulled a large bag of trail mix out of his bag to share with his fascinated hosts. They were familiar with raisins and some of the nuts, but much of the mixture was totally alien to them. However, after sampling it, they were pleased and impressed. Passing several bags of the mix to Quintus, Gabriel said, "Please accept these and divide them among your men. It is a small token of our appreciation for your help."

"Thank you," Quintus answered as he stood up and gave Gabriel a hug. "I will pass them out now, and tell the men that we expect to be here a while."

He returned shortly, and the five of them gathered around the table to sip tea and talk business.

27

Not wanting to delay their discussions, Addison quickly passed out twenty-first century teabags and pastries in the form of miniature cinnamon swirls and cake truffles. Theon, Quintus, and Avitus sampled them, commented on the teabags and the wonderful little cakes, and then turned to Addison, asking why they had returned to Alexandria.

"Gentlemen," he began, "we find ourselves getting desperate in our efforts to acquire the necessary items, and we still lack two. One is the Scroll of Fate, and we don't know where to look for it. The other missing item is an artifact with a phoenix on it. We are reasonably certain we can find this phoenix flask in Heracleion. If there is not one to be found, the artisans there should be able to make one for us. Based on our understanding of the clues we have deciphered, we believe we must have it. Therefore, we are asking for your help. We must go to Heracleion."

Avitus frowned. "This will be difficult," he said. "Zealots continue to get more out of control every day. They seem to believe that the emperor supports their violence against everything that can't be directly supported by their interpretations of Christian scriptures. We are barely managing to maintain order here. Non-Christians and Jews, considered pagans by the fanatics, are afraid to venture into the streets, and attacks against the library have increased, especially since they think all of you are taking sanctuary here. Most of the residents of the Jewish section of town have scattered for other parts of the world, and visiting men of science have left as well, since even the Christians among them are viewed suspiciously."

Looking back to Quintus and then to Gabriel and Addison, Avitus continued. "And then there are those strange beings that attacked us earlier; we have found these beings difficult to fight and would have a tough time defending you from them."

Gabriel suggested a solution. "What if we travel light and on horseback?" We could outrun the strange things. It would save a lot of time if we didn't have to fight them. And, he added, we could travel at night. You could take extra horses in case some became lame, and if you gather them at the edge of town, we could sneak out of here in the dark and join them without being seen. If they don't know we've left, they won't be ready to ambush us when we return.

"Not bad, Gabriel," Quintus answered. "You think like a military man."

Quintus and Avitus discussed the plan privately, and then Quintus told the group, "We think we can make this work. We will each provide a few men, who will depart town at different times and in different directions. We will then form up later, on the road to Heracleion, at a predetermined location. Avitus will come here after dark and escort you to the rendezvous, and hopefully you can leave without being seen."

Addison took the pouch of gold and silver and slid it to Quintus and Avitus, saying, "I don't have as much as I think you deserve, but this should at least cover the cost of this expedition."

Avitus thanked him, and answered, "You underestimate the value of this gift and of its timing. This much gold and silver will help our men and their families. And it is more than enough to purchase wagons and needed supplies, plus it will help get the families of our soldiers out of danger."

Theon had been quiet during the discussion and appeared to be upset. Addison asked him, "Do you object to this plan?"

"That isn't the reason for my mood," he answered curtly. "This venture is out of my hands. I am just reflecting on a specific aspect of the earlier discussion. It is distressing to watch as those of us who cherish knowledge and learning are disparaged as pagans. Many of us, if not most, are Christians and Jews. We believe that the advancement of knowledge is not an enemy to religion but its friend. Through learning, as we learn more about God's world, we can appreciate it better. It is really disheartening to watch this happen. My friend was murdered by those people because they saw him as a pagan, and now I am heckled whenever I leave home to come to the library. I fear that it is only a matter of time until they carry out their threats against me."

"Don't be such a pessimist," Gabriel said, trying to console Theon. Maybe this is just a passing fad and the mobs will tire of it and find a new amusement." No sooner had he spoken than he realized that he should have said nothing.

"I don't think so," responded Theon. "My daughter fears for my safety more than ever, and I feel like I must stay hidden here in the office while I hope for the rioters to end their hostility. But I don't see how that can happen.

"Already, Quintus has had to augment his soldiers, and the violence continues to grow. I had never thought that Alexandria could be destroyed from within, but it seems like that is what is happening."

Seeing Theon's distress Quintus spoke up. "We'll continue to do our best." Turning his attention to Gabriel and Addison, Quintus continued. "After the attack on Avitus's caravan, we captured and executed several of the leaders. As long as we continue to enforce law and order, we should be able to keep the peace. It will only fall apart if the mob grows bigger than we can handle."

Avitus added, "I wish to mention my thoughts about Gabriel and Shamar to all of you. The higher echelons of the Roman military used to teach their young officers about people such as them when I first began my service to Rome. We were told that the individuals who wear special robes and come at times of unrest have proven to be friends to Rome. I never thought I would see or work with anyone such as the two of them. I thought these teachings were but myths. We were never made aware of your strengths and special abilities. We were merely taught to be very respectful to you.

"We all have seen and experienced the best from each of you. We understand from your actions that you are true friends of the Roman soldiers, their leadership, and their families. This is why we will try to always accommodate you to the best of our ability."

With that said, he rose, followed by Quintus, and the two men headed to the door. Quintus turned back to face Gabriel and Addison and said, "We thank you for your hospitality, but we must gather our party and begin dispersing our people so they can make the rendezvous. Please let us out, Theon." They bowed, and Theon unlocked the door.

Four

Heracleion

Wagons were lined up full of families and provisions long before the sky showed even a hint of dawn. Anxious mothers tearfully said their good-byes to soldiers and tried to put cranky children back to sleep.

The plan had changed. Because of the unexpected influx of cash from Addison, wagons had been purchased to help evacuate the soldiers' families, which would also be used to provide cover for Gabriel and Addison. Gabriel and Addison were to hide within the wagons as they departed, and there would be no need to explain extra guards and horses, as onlookers would assume everything there was in support of the families.

The soldiers appreciated Addison's generous offering and actually competed for the honor of escorting Addison and Gabriel to Heracleion.

Avitus approached Addison and Gabriel as they sat innocuously beside two of the women who were driving some of the wagons. He said, "Theon matched your donation, so we were able to get provisions for our journey as well. The men appreciate what you and Theon have done and owe you a debt that can only be repaid with their thanks.

"Theon packed your provisions in saddlebags on the two horses tied to the wagons, so you can ride once we have departed the city. We will be leaving very soon because we must be on the way before the sun rises and the younger children wake up."

Soon the three large wagons began moving, slowly squeaking and creaking their way out of the city, accompanied by a small contingent of guards. Most of the guards were Avitus's hired men, who would continue with the wagons to protect the families from being captured for ransom or slavery. The soldiers who stayed behind waved as their loved ones slowly disappeared into the darkness.

The women were solemn and said nothing, occasionally waving to the men behind them until they could no longer be seen.

A few hours later, as the eastern sky began to glow and children began waking up, the wagons stopped, and a few hidden soldiers hopped out. They mounted some of the horses, and Gabriel and Addison joined them. Avitus gathered the men who would continue onward with Gabriel and Addison, and provided some last-minute instructions. "Don't dally and return as quickly as you can and keep a watchful eye out for bandits or those strange creatures. Don't fight if you can avoid it. Once you're done with this errand, try and catch up with us to help out."

Addison and Gabriel followed the escort on toward Heracleion at a somewhat faster pace, staring ahead as the sky transitioned through various shades of pink until the orange ball of the sun pushed its way above the horizon and then became too bright to look at. It had been years since Addison had been on a horse, and it wasn't long before he regretted leaving the wagon.

Well after daybreak the party stopped, and the horses were fed and watered while everyone rested. Gabriel laughed when he saw they were using some of the water bottles that had been brought in the footlocker on their earlier trip. "I wonder how this will be explained," he joked, "centuries from now when archeologists find those. They will think their site has been contaminated. I don't think those decompose very fast."

Well before lunchtime they arrived on the shore across from the island city of Heracleion. One of the men dismounted and began searching in the reeds. Avitus had made arrangements for a small boat to be hidden there for the two travelers to use. Luckily it was still there. He pointed out the island that would be most likely to have a glassmaker and drew a map in the dirt. The two men prepared to get into the boat.

One of the men whistled to get their attention. "Don't go yet," he said. "Avitus sent some more appropriate clothing for you to wear over those odd clothes you are wearing."

"Please tell me what we are dressed as," asked Addison, while the men helped them get changed.

"These clothes will make you look like well-to-do merchants," said one of the soldiers. Tell them you are from Taposiris and your mother sent you here to get a phoenix design in a double-glazed flask to be buried in her grave with her when she dies." Seeing their puzzled faces, he added, "This is a normal custom. When people pass on, their families sometimes decorate their graves with beautiful glass items. Say that her sister was buried with one and so she wants one too."

They faced each other, and Gabriel smirked. "This is like Halloween," he remarked.

Addison answered, "This is only temporary, and I will keep telling myself that."

They returned to the boat, and Gabriel suggested that Addison get in and sit down. After the boat was stable, Gabriel pushed it off the bank and jumped in. He rowed in the direction shown him by the soldier. It took longer than they had expected, but they finally arrived at their destination. Gabriel jumped ashore and dragged the boat onto the bank and then helped Addison disembark.

People were staring at them when they arrived. Apparently, this wasn't the way most rich merchants traveled. "Never mind them," Addison said. "Just try and blend in." Gabriel tied the boat to a stake in the ground.

Some were laughing when they moved up into the area. One of the men said, "You must be strangers here. Most people pull their boats up to the docks just beyond that building over there," pointing to a building about fifty yards away.

"Thanks," Addison said. "We'll remember that next time. Unfortunately, we are in a bit of a hurry."

"I feel stupid," said Gabriel quietly.

"Don't worry about it," Addison answered. "Just keep trying to blend in, and watch for a glass shop."

This did appear to be a market area, so they began walking down the street, looking into each shop as they progressed. The area was clean and orderly, and all the shops seemed to be open for business, with samples of their wares on display. But they saw no glass or any hint that there might be a glassblower in town.

At the end of the street, Gabriel continued to follow Addison down the next street one block over. It still was not looking promising, and they began getting nervous.

Finally, on a third street, they found a shop with glass items on display. This street was a little dirty and less organized, but they approached the shop, went up a couple of stairs, and entered the store.

Addison breathed a sigh of relief. The room was clean, and the shelves were stocked with a wide assortment of glassware. The proprietor approached and asked if he could help.

Addison explained that their mother had to have a double-glazed flask with a phoenix design on it for her grave, and it had to be similar to one that was buried with her sister. "We need it soon, since we are only here for a day," he added.

The man frowned and quipped, "Just take the dead woman's. Nobody will know."

Shocked, Addison answered, "We can't do that. Our mother will want to see it, and she will know.

The man was quiet as he surveyed them. It was obvious that he didn't want to do the work. "I hope you don't want this today," he said. "It will take the rest of the day just to make the flask and most of the night to add the design. I'll have to burn oil all night, which is expensive, and in the low light of an oil lamp, I can't make a flawless picture. My father made one just like you described a few years ago, and he is much better at it than I am. He'll be back next week. Why don't you come back then?"

"We need this as a surprise for our mother this week," Addison said. "We will pay for your oil, and we will pay extra for the inconvenience of staying up all night."

With that, the vendor's eyes lit up. "I can do my best to make what you want," he said. "It will not be as good as the one my father made, and it will cost more because it is a rush job. I'll make it today and put the design on it tonight. It will be ready in the morning."

Addison was disappointed. He had not anticipated waiting so long for a flask to be made. Pausing, he realized he was in another time period and everything would take longer. *Of course! It just took us nearly all day to go twenty-five miles.*

He was at a disadvantage in haggling over the price. He didn't have any idea what the going rate was for glassware, and even if he had, he didn't know the value of the currency he had brought from Avitus. "I am about to buy the Brooklyn Bridge," he whispered to Gabriel. He pulled some coins from his pouch and held them out for the merchant to see. The merchant looked horrified, so he pulled out some more. The merchant seemed to glance at his pouch to judge how many more coins might be in it, and Addison took out a few more coins and put the pouch away. *These coins are gold. They have to be worth several hundred dollars each in our time.*

Seeing the pouch going back into a pocket, the merchant understood the subtle hint, and agreed. Addison said, "Half now and half tomorrow." They had a deal.

Addison then asked if there was anything he or Gabriel could do to expedite the process.

"No" was the answer. "Just go away and come back tomorrow morning."

As they departed, Gabriel asked, "What's to keep him from pocketing the money and hiding until we're gone?"

"Greed," answered Addison. "I believe we just paid far more than it is worth, and he will be expecting that much again. And, we can expect to be overwhelmed by merchants when we return tomorrow, if experience is any guide."

"What experience?" Gabriel asked.

"I have dealt with these guys' descendants. I know how they are."

"Is that why you are so upset?" Gabriel asked.

"I didn't know it was that obvious," answered Addison. "No not at all. In a deal where you don't know the value of the merchandise and you don't know the value of the currency, you must expect to be gouged. I'm not happy because I didn't want to have to wait an extra day. Chances are, he won't be ready by morning, and we could be here all day."

As they walked back toward the boat, a merchant approached and asked if they would like to sample his cheese. After a slight hesitation, Addison agreed to follow the man back to his shop to see what he had to offer. The shop was very clean, and they both enjoyed the aroma of food that was being prepared. A woman joined the man and proudly showed them their foodstuffs. Addison purchased some wheat cakes, cheese, and meat that had just been prepared. The woman packaged the hot meat in a ceramic bowl and wrapped the cheese and wheat cakes in a cloth and tied it up. "I think the boys will like this," Addison said to Gabriel.

As they reentered the street, Addison looked around and saw a shop that piqued his interest. He pointed to the shop and asked Gabriel to join him. It was a jewelry store, and Gabriel couldn't imagine why they needed to stop here. Addison said he would explain later.

The shopkeeper approached Addison and asked if he could assist him in finding anything. Addison described what he was looking for, and the man informed him that a similar ring was across the room in his display of *specialty* merchandise. Addison took note of the emphasis on the word "specialty" and knew he meant "higher-priced items."

Gabriel and Addison followed. It took Addison a New York second to see what Shamar had described to him. Pointing to the ring and asking the appropriate questions, Addison and the merchant came to an agreement.

Addison and Gabriel watched as the merchant packaged the ring in a special wooden box that he next sealed shut with wax and then dipped the box into the wax.

Waiting but a moment for the wax to dry, Addison thanked the merchant, made a payment, took the waxed box, and left the shop, this time heading for their boat. Along the way Addison explained, "Shamar wanted me to ask Avitus about purchasing a special ring to present to Sophia when he proposed marriage, and this is the type of place and ring that Avitus suggested."

Gabriel agreed that the ring was beautiful. "I wonder how they engraved a moon and the three stars on the hematite? And each star has a different colored gem in its center, adding to its eloquent beauty. I think Sophia will be very impressed with her engagement ring."

"I understand," said Addison, "that the hematite, according to Greek legend, represents the blood and love that flows from the ring through the ring finger to the heart of she who wears it. And the moon represents a divine sign of Israel, and the stars symbolize honor, a guiding force, and good luck."

They got into the boat and returned to the soldiers, and both were still in awe of the aquatic life serenely drifting by, birds, hippos, and crocodiles all at peace with one another.

The men were surprised to see them return so soon but were delighted that he had brought samples of the local cuisine. Addison explained that they had to spend the night, and the soldiers, disappointed, found a place to camp.

"We will break camp when you return to the city, and we can leave for home as soon as you get back with your merchandise," said the soldier in charge. Addison thanked them.

Addison went to his horse and placed the waxed box in his saddlebag for safe keeping.

The next day they found their way back to the shop and knocked at the door, hearing activity inside. The man slowly opened the door and welcomed them back. It was obvious that he had not had much sleep, if any. They walked over to a table, where the man apologetically showed them the flask, disappointed in his work because of the rush. Addison could see that it was truly a work of art and expressed his pleasure, thanked him, and paid the man. The flask was exactly what he had ordered.

They began their trek back to the boat but were intercepted by another merchant. He introduced himself and invited them to his shop. "I sell fine linens of the best quality," he said, "but I have never seen cloth like you are wearing," pointing to Gabriel's robe that hung under the hem of his clothes.

Gabriel looked down but was not quick enough to stop the man from reaching down and stroking the robe. Gabriel felt a slight tingle run through his body. The snake had been awakened by the merchant's touch, and Gabriel didn't know what to expect next.

The merchant paused for a moment and glanced into Gabriel's eyes. Then he offered to buy Gabriel's robe, and when he was turned down, he offered more.

Addison pushed his way between the two and interjected. "I'm sorry, but we must hurry home. The robe is not for sale."

"This is bad," he told Gabriel. "One merchant thinks we have more money than we know how to spend, and another is offering a small fortune for your robe. It is imperative that we get out of here soon and make all haste in getting home. We are begging to be robbed and perhaps worse."

They hurried to the boat, where Gabriel untied it and pushed them off from the wharf. While Addison watched to see whether they were followed, Gabriel jumped into the boat and rowed as fast as he could, pulling the oars until his arms ached.

As they neared the far shore close to the soldiers, the boat suddenly lurched into the sky, seeming to have a life of its own. They had collided with a hippo! One side of the boat lifted high over their heads and then continued rolling over until it had dumped them into the river. Seeing Addison going down, Gabriel swam over to him and grabbed his collar, which he could barely see in the muddy water. He wrapped his arm around Addison's chest and began pulling him toward the shore.

Swimming in clothes was not easy, but Gabriel dared not risk losing them. Things were flying by his head as he approached the shore, and he realized that they were arrows. *What are they shooting at? Arrows won't stop a hippo.* The men helped pull Addison to shore, and Gabriel noticed that Addison had lost the flask.

As he dived back into the river, Gabriel could hear the men yelling at him, but he couldn't understand what they were saying. He waved at them and yelled back, "I'll be right back. I have to get the flask." He swam over to the boat and dipped under it to see if he could find the flask. He thought he saw a sight movement down near the bottom and gulped some air and dived down to investigate. The visibility was poor. He felt around the mud at the bottom and finally found it. With his lungs about to burst, he shot back to the surface toward the boat. But it wasn't the boat. It was a hippo.

He stopped his ascent and struggled to change direction, but another shadow appeared in front of him, not as big as a hippo. *A crocodile!* Having nowhere to go, he inhaled some water in his surprise and felt excruciating pain throughout his chest. As his vision faded, he thought he saw an old shepherd in robes in the water poking the hippo with his staff near the crocodile, and the hippo turning on the reptile. Next the shepherd went to Gabriel and whispered to him, "You have the scroll of fate," then gently pushed him toward the water's surface.

Gabriel awoke on shore, as men were forcing water out of his lungs and letting air back in. He looked at his hand and was relieved to see that he had not dropped the flask. Unable to talk, he looked around for the old man who had saved his life but didn't see him anywhere.

Seeing that Gabriel was conscious, the men pulled him to his feet and forcefully moved him toward his horse, and helped him onto it. As he was getting seated in the saddle, he looked back and saw a couple of other hippos joining the fight with the crocodile. They seemed to be taking turns grabbing the beast's body in their huge mouths as they dragged the poor animal to shore. There still was no sign of the old man.

"That could have been you!" exclaimed one of the soldiers. "What were you thinking?"

"I got the flask," he gasped, still trying to recover his breath.

"Those hippos will kill that crocodile," the soldier said. "And they could have killed you just as easily. They typically drag the crocodiles onto the shore and then stomp them until they're crushed. And with their poor eyesight, they would have easily mistaken you for a crocodile."

By the time they stopped for a break, Gabriel and Addison had dried in the warm air. The soldiers fed and watered the horses, and then they rested too. Noticing that Addison was unusually quiet, Gabriel asked what was wrong. He normally had comments for everything that they passed.

"I'm afraid the water might have ruined the contents of the flask."

They both examined it. "The stopper seems to be secure, and I don't see any cracks," Gabriel said. "We might know for certain once we get back."

They pressed on.

They hurried, giving broad berth to all other travelers they saw and resting in wide spaces that were safe from ambush. They finally reached Alexandria late in the evening and were welcomed back by Quintus.

They rested in the barracks with the men, where Gabriel had gained even higher status. Not only could he fight the strange creatures and rioting zealots, but now he was a hippo fighter. He smiled and then slept very soundly.

After breakfast, they all gathered at Theon's office to say good-bye again.

"You are lucky to be alive," Quintus told Gabriel. "Hippos are dangerous when they're mad. They can travel faster than you in water and on land, and they are mean and deadly. He then smiled at Gabriel and, with a chuckle in his voice, said, "I understand my men refer to you as the Hippo Fighter."

They exchanged pleasantries, and Gabriel gave Quintus a big hug and thanked him and his men for all they had done to assist in their adventurers. He told Quintus that he would miss him, Avitus, and their men but would never forget them. Showing reluctance to leave, Gabriel turned to Addison and wrapped him in the robe. Standing tall and waving a final good-bye to Quintus, Gabriel gave a salute, then together they departed for modern-day Denver.

Five

Vincent Leaves for Alexandria

S he still hadn't arrived, and the plane was ready. Vincent wasn't surprised, but he was disappointed, and frightened. He knew most of Senka's mistakes were his responsibility, and he knew the phantom knew that as well. Unless he could turn this fiasco around, his fate would be far worse than hers.

Finally giving up on her last-second arrival, he told the security detail to board the corporate jet and told the pilot to get moving. After reminding the security guards to expect a long flight, he ordered a good stiff drink to be delivered as soon as possible after takeoff.

Even while the plane was taxiing, he continued to watch for Senka, hoping to see her running for the departing jet.

The takeoff was smooth, and his drink was delivered after the seatbelt sign was extinguished. He sipped it for a while as he went over his plan. After landing they would find and watch the Daniels group until the watchman appeared. If possible, they would help the watchman to disappear without a trace, so no one would know what had happened to him. If this was too hard, they would just have him killed openly. As far as anyone knew, that would end the danger, since there could no longer be a ceremony.

However, just to be certain, they would then follow the group until the locations of the stone and all or most of the flasks and robes could be determined.

Then, in one coordinated operation, those would all be confiscated. That part shouldn't be too hard. They were only four men and two women, and most were weak and had no fighting skills. Then everything would be presented to his master, and all would be forgiven.

His mind returned to Senka. He had been fond of her, and he regretted that she had been removed from the team. Thinking that he would probably never see her again, he returned his glass and, with a shaking hand, ordered another drink—bigger and stronger than the first.

▲　▲　▲

Returning to twenty-first century Denver, Addison and Gabriel were surprised to see Eli in the office-apartment. "I'm glad to see you're safe, but why are you here?" asked Addison. "You should be in Alexandria, helping Sophia and Shamar. They shouldn't be there alone."

Eli became defensive immediately, and Addison and Gabriel could see he was prepared to justify his and Mariah's actions. "Sit down," directed Eli. "There is a lot we need to talk about. To answer your first question, Mariah is very sick, and we have been at the hospital."

And then he proceeded to tell them about the events from their arrival in New York to the present. "We need to change our plans," he added. "Someone has to stay with Mariah until she gets back on her feet."

With a great sigh, Addison apologized and went to the kitchen, knowing the mundane task of preparing tea and snacks would allow him to concentrate. He was worried about Mariah's symptoms and how fast they had developed. He was also concerned that her symptoms were so similar to those of the disease that had killed Edward. *Eli is right. Our plans have to be changed.*

Addison carried the tray of tea to the table, and he began by saying, "It appears that evil has found a way to slow us down, although I don't understand how anyone could have done this to Mariah deliberately. She is so kind to everyone."

Changing the subject Addison stated, "We need to gather our thoughts. I think we are missing something. Apparently, Rabbi Katz went back to ancient

Alexandria several times. What is odd to me is that none of the people we met there ever ran into him. How is it that he seems to have visited the two secret rooms but never met Theon?"

"Maybe the rabbi met with the Jews," Gabriel piped in. "There was a big Jewish community, but there might not be now, since they're all leaving."

Both men looked at each other, astonished. "Of course!" shouted Addison. "Why didn't we think of that? The rabbi might have learned something about the gem or the other artifacts from the rabbi in ancient Alexandria. We need to go back now, before they're all gone. We must find out what the rabbi learned from them."

"You're right," Eli said. "I'm ashamed to say that we never thought to look up the Jewish community. Even though Shamar and Sophia did in Taposiris, I failed to do so because it didn't occur to me to do that in Alexandra."

"I think I need to go," said Eli, "since I can relate to them better. One of you needs to stay with Mariah. I would prefer to take Gabriel, since it has become so dangerous."

"Sounds like we have a plan," said Addison. "Since the Jews are all going on a long journey, I wonder whether you could take some food with you, as an offer to show your appreciation for their help. Let's go by a store and pick up some nuts and dried fruits."

"We might really impress them if we could bring some modern treats, such as bottled water and freeze-dried ice cream," Gabriel added.

"I don't think so," Eli answered. "That might be a little too much of a culture shock."

Addison quickly said that he disagreed. "Eli, when we took provisions with us to ancient Alexandria Avitus, Quintus and the soldiers were all surprised at what we brought. Yet Sophia mentioned to us in her examination of the rabbi's personal book keeping that he had taken substantial food stuffs with him somewhere. Therefore I believe the rabbi took food with him to ancient Alexandria for the Jews he was working with, and we should do the same."

Thinking for a short moment, Eli said, "Gabriel, we need to go shopping."

After Gabriel and Addison returned from the store, Eli looked in on Mariah. Not wanting to wake her, he asked Addison to give her his love and explain what they were doing. Gabriel left his robe with Addison, and Eli and Gabriel wrapped in Eli's robe and left.

Left alone with his thoughts, Addison began fixing a meal for Mariah, hoping she would wake up soon; however, depressing memories of Edward's suffering with a condition that was so like Mariah's frightened him.

Six

Vincent Loses a Partner

Sago was amazed that he had not been discovered since infiltrating Vincent's team of guards. He had gambled that they had come from several different sections of the organization and didn't know each other. So far he hadn't been recognized and had managed to get included with the special team going to Egypt. Luckily, his disguises included fake passports. Still, he kept a low profile and avoided Vincent, since discovery would mean instant death.

As Sago loosened his safety belt for the long trip, he saw, in the forward part of the cabin, Vincent staring at the empty seat in front of him. "Looks like he's worried about a no-show," Sago speculated.

From his seat, he could overhear some of Vincent's advisors filling him in on Senka, who apparently had made a number of enemies at high levels, and some of her rivals were pressing to have an example made of her following her failure. *So, she's going down too. That didn't take long. The empty seat must be hers.*

After a long flight, he could see Vincent receiving information from the aircrew, probably telling him they were about to land. He seemed to be checking his mobile devices for situation updates.

Vincent stood and addressed the detail. "I want the main part of the team assigned to finding Shamar and Sophia for interrogation. That will be their only priority.

"We believe they are in Alexandria, possibly near some of the ancient ruins. I am passing out special cell phones that relay all voice and text communications from Eli to any of the others in his group. Pay attention to those, since we will be able to capture everyone's phone numbers and locations as Eli's contacts reply to him. Keep a record of those, as they will be useful to our IT department. And don't accidently send a text back to them. We don't want to tip them off."

Sago took one of the phones and studied it, checking for messages and past calls. He needed to get one of the other guard's phones and would take care of that as soon as he found a guard alone. When the party departed the plane, he integrated himself into the search team and struck up a conversation with one of the other members.

▲ ▲ ▲

Eli and Gabriel landed again near Pompey's Pillar in ancient Alexandria. Gabriel awoke first, to the strong smell of alcohol and someone shaking him vigorously.

"Hey you, wake up!" said the voice that was attached to the boozed breath. "Don't you remember my warning from last time I found you? Get up and get out of here"

Gabriel thanked him and pushed him away, and woke up Addison. None of Quintus's or Avitus's men were around, so they hooked towing straps to the box of supplies and departed in the direction of the library, both men feeling insecure without a familiar face around.

Just short of the library, they finally encountered some of the soldiers, who recognized them and escorted them the rest of the way. Approaching Theon's office they were shocked to see Quintus in civilian clothing.

"I've retired," Quintus said, upon seeing their surprise. "It seems that we are now expected to enforce laws only when it is convenient for the emperor and ignore the law and give sanctuary to lawbreakers when they are persecuting non-Christians. The resulting riots are so dangerous now that even some Christians are leaving for fear that they might be mistaken for apostates or heretics.

"You are lucky to have found us. We should be leaving soon to join our families, which, thanks to you, have found safe havens in other villages far from here and the surrounding danger."

Walking up to Gabriel, Quintus gave him a big hug and said, "I am so glad to see you once again. You have been on my mind of late, and I have missed speaking with you and Shamar. Avitus misses you too, as we both take pleasure in recalling our time spent with you. You are both thought of as our brothers and respected as family.

You should know that our families are heading west to Cyrene and then to Leptis Magna and from there we move together through El Djem, Dougga, and to our final destination, Tipasa. Perhaps someday we might meet you again."

Eli quickly spoke up. "We came back to visit the Jewish community. Can you help us find them?"

Avitus was not encouraging. "The Jews have almost all left. I think there might be a few families remaining, including their rabbi and his brother, who both stayed long enough to make sure everyone else was able to safely flee. I respect them for that. I could take you there, but it would be dangerous. The crowds are totally uncontrollable now. We'll send an escort to get him and bring him here."

"We brought some supplies to help them on their travel," said Eli. "If there are only two families left, we have too much. Perhaps we could leave the excess with you, Quintus and Avitus, to help your men with your travels."

They knocked on Theon's door, which, with a familiar click, was unlocked after a long wait. Theon was shocked to see them but gladly welcomed them in and gave each of them a big hug. "I'm really grateful that I can see you one more time, but you must finish your business and leave quickly. The crowds are larger and more violent. They will certainly kill you," he said, pointing to Gabriel.

The men helped carry the supplies into his office, and Theon locked the door behind them. Eli then supervised the division of the supplies, setting aside one large box for the rabbi's and his brother's families, and then packing two more boxes for Avitus, Quintus, and their men.

While they waited, Quintus provided more detail about his retirement. Following several incidents in which Quintus had punished lawbreakers, complaints had been submitted about his conduct, so Quintus and his men had been relieved of duty. Pausing for a moment, Quintus explained what he thought the consequences of the emperor's actions would cause. "There will be total anarchy now, and I can't imagine how the streets will improve after I'm gone. Avitus and his men have chosen to wait and accompany me and my remaining men when we leave Alexandria for good."

Quintus exhibited mixed emotions about leaving at a time when the people of Alexandria would need his protection, but he would have been very frustrated in not being allowed to restore order. He was grateful that he was joining Avitus's men and their large brotherhood. Turning his attention to Theon, he said, "You should come with us."

"I will miss you, my friend," Theon said. "I wish I could join you, but I must stay and protect the library. Once this is all over, they will need the knowledge within this compound and my head to help restore the world to normal. Besides, all my life's work is here, as well as a lifetime of memories."

It wasn't long after that that the rabbi arrived with a couple of Quintus's men. "I was told that you wanted to see me before I left," the rabbi said. "How may I be of assistance, Quintus?"

Eli presented the rabbi with the supplies he had brought. At first the rabbi was dumbfounded but assumed it was a gift from Rabbi Katz.

"What a blessing you have brought," the rabbi said. "I thank you, and my brother thanks you as well. Is this from Rabbi Katz? It looks just like the gifts he had brought us in the past. Please thank him for his generosity; it is appreciated. I must go now, but I wish you Godspeed in your journey."

"Wait!" Eli said. He thought for a moment as to how to present the sad information about Rabbi Katz's death to the rabbi.

The rabbi turned to see why he had been commanded to stop. He politely waited for Eli to speak.

"I'm afraid I have bad news," Eli said. "Rabbi Katz has passed away, but I am trying to continue his work, and I desperately need to learn everything he learned and did here in Alexandria."

The rabbi's demeanor immediately changed, and he became solemn but appeared to be anxious about something that he obviously was reluctant to share in front of a crowd. He turned to Avitus and very respectfully asked, "Could you please ask your men to take us back to my home? I have something for Eli, and it is very important that he come get it."

Avitus motioned to a couple of the men, and they grabbed the rabbi's gifts from Eli to carry for him.

The men departed with his supplies, and then waited for Eli and the rabbi, preparing to escort them. Turning to Eli the rabbi said, "Come with me, my friend. We have much to discuss on the way to my home."

Looking back at Avitus, the rabbi said, "I'll send Eli and your men back shortly. I thank you all for helping, and may God shine his light upon you all. Quintus, I bid you farewell and wish you the same blessing I gave Avitus. You have been the finest protector of Alexandria and its inhabitants, and especially the large Jewish community who called this place home. Thank you."

Surprised by this turn of events, Eli looked blankly at everyone in the room and turned to follow. Quintus saw Eli's concern and added reassuringly, "We will wait for you, my friend."

Then, venturing to the remaining supplies and turning to Gabriel, Quintus said, "Is there tea and some of those delicious small cakes in here?" Everyone laughed, and tea and cakes were divided up among everyone present.

Following their escort, the rabbi and Eli remained slightly behind in order to have a private conversation. "I'm sorry to hear that Rabbi Katz can no longer continue with his work," the rabbi began, sounding very concerned. "He had anticipated his demise and told me that if it happened, it would be important for the future of humankind for me to pass on something that he left with me for safekeeping. That is one of the reasons I stayed behind when our people left. Without him, this project is at great risk, but it is so important that you assume the task and make every effort to succeed. He left one item for me to give you. I don't believe there is anything further that I can do to assist you; however, if you should seek me again, I will help as much as I can."

The rabbi said no more for the remainder of the trip to his house. The silence made the distance seem further than it actually was, but Eli didn't know what to say or what help to ask for. Then a thought crossed his mind. *Could it be he is silent because he doesn't want to be overheard, or maybe he thinks I know everything I need to know?* Eli was puzzled.

A fully loaded wagon sat in front of the rabbi's house, with two women and a man standing near it, prepared for travel. While the much-appreciated supplies were added to the rest of the cargo, the rabbi introduced his brother, sister-in-law, and then his wife, who all began thanking the men for helping. The rabbi's wife said that the entire community was sorry to see Quintus's soldiers and Avitus's mercenaries leave and even sorrier that their service had not been appreciated as of late.

As everyone waited by the wagon, the rabbi motioned for Eli to join him, and soon they both disappeared into his home. Walking to a particular area, the rabbi removed several bricks from their setting and placed them on the floor. Then he put his arm deep into the opened area, placing his arm well into the hole, and withdrew a purple pouch.

Gently handing the pouch to Eli, the rabbi asked him to delay for a moment. The rabbi busied himself with replacing the bricks and then turned to face Eli. "This belongs to the shomer. Guard it with your life, and give it only to him. Don't let anyone know that you possess it. Just give it to him as it is right now. God bless you, and I pray for your success. I am glad that you were able to speak with me because this secret hiding place was only known to me and Rabbi Katz, and that you knew about Rabbi Katz's task was noteworthy to me."

As the rabbi and Eli exited his home, the women saw the beautifully decorated pouch, and they immediately began whispering to each other in soft but excited voices.

The rabbi then turned from Eli and Avitus's men and, with his brother and the two women, mounted the wagon and drove away. As they were leaving, they all turned and waved.

Eli waved back, wondering how they would fare as they departed this hostile former home and ventured forward, seeking a new life.

Eli glanced down at the pouch he held and then over at Avitus's men, who stood silent and motionless. Eli realized that he had become an important courier. He continued to watch the wagon until it disappeared. One of the soldiers tapped him on the shoulder and asked whether everything was all right.

"Yes," he said.

"Shall we return to Theon's office?" asked the soldier.

"Please lead the way," responded Eli.

They looked at each other, and with Eli between them, they made their way through the streets back to the library.

As they walked, one of them said, "I'm glad that you and Gabriel returned in time to say good-bye. It is unfortunate that he didn't have a chance to teach us his unusual method of fighting."

Then he continued, wistfully looking around, "I'm going to miss walking the streets and looking after the people of this fine city. But being able to continue on with Quintus and Avitus will make our transition into civilian life and a new career easier."

Seven

DENVER DETECTIVES WORK WITH INTERPOL

In all his time with the police department, Tony De La Garza had never met anyone from INTERPOL. Until today it had only been something he had heard about in training and seen in movies.

After exiting the parking garage at the Denver airport, Tony made his way to arrivals. He would be working with Mr. Don Wellington, who had just flown in from Great Britain, stopping in New York only to change flights and clear customs. He checked arrivals and saw the flight from New York City was on time.

He stopped for coffee while he waited. The reason Tony remained involved with the case was because the INTERPOL's suspects happened to be the same people he had just arrested and interviewed a few days ago. He thought back about the incident with Eli and Mariah Daniels and their friend Addison. He remembered warning them to be careful when he released them from custody, since it was obvious to him that someone was trying to get the three of them detained for some unknown reason. The justification for this INTERPOL visit was instigated by someone providing an anonymous tip that Addison had stolen archeological treasures.

Tony thought it was unlikely that the Daniels or Addison would steal, but Mr. Wellington had sufficient cause to investigate, so Tony decided to keep an open mind.

Still nervous about meeting this guest, he realized they had not made any arrangements for where to meet. Tony checked the arrivals screen again. Trying to determine which luggage carousel was serving Mr. Wellington's flight, he headed down there, expecting no trouble in finding him since he had his photograph. Tony rechecked the information on his guest to secure his cell phone number and discovered all his numbers were international numbers. "Great," he remarked. "I should have brought a sign with his name in large print."

The sign over the carousel lit up with the flight number, and the carousel began moving. Even though most of the people rushed to the luggage, he could still see their faces well enough to know that his subject was not among them. As he studied them, he heard his name called from behind. Turning, he was surprised to see his target already carrying his luggage.

"Hi," he said, smiling. "I'm Donald Wellington. I presume you are Tony De La Garza. I normally travel light and have no checked bags. I packed carefully, making sure I didn't pack any shampoos big enough to blow up a plane, and no weapons."

Tony asked if he would like to stop for something to eat or go straight to his hotel and eat later.

"I'll eat later" was the reply.

"I'm surprised that you came all the way from England," Tony said as he greeted the INTERPOL agent. "I didn't think you folks took vague, anonymous tips so seriously."

"We normally don't," Wellington answered. "We intended not to act on it at first. Although there had been a controversy about some minor items that were lost, no one was aware of any major disappearances.

"But then after some initial inquiries, we discovered some oddities. When we tried to contact the people involved with the expedition in question, we found that Edward Knight died some years ago, and Rabbi Katz, who funded a majority of this archeological dig, died days ago.

Then when we tried to follow up with three others who were involved with the dig in Alexandria, Egypt, we learned that they have all disappeared, strangely, around the exact same time very recently.

Mr. Knight's butler, Addison Richardson, has not answer any calls, and Mr. and Mrs. Daniels are not at home or at work, and Mr. Daniels's staff at the museum where he works is very secretive about his status."

"Funny you should say that," Tony remarked. "The Daniels and Mr. Richards were detained in the past week in an incident in which they were being framed for a robbery that allegedly involved the Daniels's car. They were cooperative, but they never told us where they were staying."

"Wow," Wellington said. "That's one more reason to come here, had we known.

"But there's more. We learned, or rather were informed, that several artifacts that might have come from the Alexandria site in question were discovered at the deceased rabbi's home and have been transferred to a museum in New York. Then, oddly enough, several days after Mr. Daniels disappeared, he showed up at the New York museum to view the rabbi's contraband. We followed up on his visit to the New York Museum and saw him on video.

"Regardless of the merit of the tip, it is obvious that something strange is happening. Since I can't reach any of them, we decided it would be best to come here and see what's up and speak to you and hopefully them in person."

After checking the agent into the hotel, they made their way to Tony's office, where they began discussing the case over a bag of burgers and fries they had picked up on the way.

"Here's the file I have on your suspects from that incident a few days ago," Tony began. "A witness to a robbery provided a detailed description of the Daniels's car, to include a license number, so we brought the Daniels in for questioning. Actually it turned out to be Mariah Daniels and the butler, Addison.

"However, the car in the robbery video was not their car; the Daniels's car had been in a repair shop in another city. The car in the robbery had been a stolen car, and the car bore only a slight resemblance to the Daniels's car. And the witness was bogus. It seemed obvious to us that someone just wanted them detained by the police, although no one knows why."

"Do you think this could be another red herring?" Donald asked. "Possibly to use the police to harass the family again?"

"I have no idea," Tony replied. "We should know more when we visit Patrick Knight's mansion, where Addison is employed and lives. We shouldn't need a warrant, since we are only asking questions. Besides, he is the butler and seems to be efficient and straightforward. I don't anticipate any problems."

Donald thought for a moment and asked, "Is he a real English butler?"

"So I've been told," said Tony.

Following the discussion they departed for Patrick's mansion.

The house was situated in a beautiful neighborhood with well-kept elegant houses on large lots. "What a gorgeous mansion," Donald commented. "Except for the mountain range in the distance, it could pass for an English manor house."

Pulling up to the porch, they exited the car and rang the doorbell, and rang it again when there was no answer.

Tony said, "Let's walk around the property and see if he's in the garden. I remember that Addison had said that he enjoyed gardening."

The gate was open, and on the gate they noticed stains on the door that looked like a bloody handprint. Tony and Donald leaned back in unison, gazed into each other's faces, and then moved carefully to avoid touching anything. Tony placed is hands in his pockets and asked Donald to do the same, just to make sure they did not contaminate anything. Next Tony stepped in front of Donald and led the way into the backyard.

"What a wonderful garden," whispered Donald. "It clearly has received a lot of care." Donald was amazed at the landscaping. He stared in awe at the craftsmanship and design of this area. Some of the landscape seemed Egyptian but much appeared to be English. He pointed out to Tony that the flowers hanging on the wall were wisteria, which is an English tradition in many mansions with gardens, and the trees on the opposite side were yew. This family definitely had a flare for English design.

While Tony was surveying the pots of wisteria, an anomaly in the garden wall caught his attention. "I think there's something odd about that wall," Tony said. "It has been cracked or moved," he said, and they approached it.

As they drew near, they noticed that a portion of the wall had swung open, as though it were a door. "This looks like a hidden entrance to a cellar," commented Donald.

Then they were both overcome by a very strong stench, and both men recognized the smell of death. They buried their faces in their jackets to minimize the smell as they approached. The opening was beginning to look like an entrance to an underground room.

Tony said, "I should learn whether this is human or animal before I call it in. The smell is definitely coming from this opened door."

"Given the circumstances," Donald quickly responded, "I think you need backup. I think we got the tip because someone wanted you to find whoever is dead at the bottom of the stairs, rather than anything about old treasures. Possibly Mr. Addison Richardson or the owner of this domicile, Mr. Patrick Knight, as neither one seems to be around."

"I certainly hope not," said Tony as he retrieved his cell phone. "Addison seemed like such a nice man." He then contacted his office and requested more officers.

As they waited for more men, they walked around the house peeking into windows, looking for footprints that might indicate a break-in, and concluded that the house was probably not occupied.

Soon a team of police, Tony's boss, and a few other detectives showed up. The police donned masks and descended the stairs, while Tony and Donald briefed the others on what they knew of the situation.

After the police had been in the cellar for a short while, one of them called Tony, saying, "I think you need to see this."

After putting on protective clothing and masks, they entered the bunker. Each was amazed at the bunker's size as well as the fact that such a large facility could be so well hidden on the estate. Tony said to Donald, "This must be the hidden room that someone had mentioned to you."

An officer at the bottom of the stairs showed them the surveillance equipment and television monitors, saying to Tony, "We need warrants for this entire bunker, to include all the surveillance equipment and any tapes. And I think those warrants need to cover the house too."

He then turned to Donald, and said, "Agent Wellington, we would like to show you what we found in a glass case. I believe it pertains to what you were sent here to investigate."

"Go on ahead," Tony said to Donald. "I have to see and make notes for everything they need the warrant for."

The coroner arrived while Tony was studying the surveillance equipment, and Tony quickly followed the coroner and officer to the room with the body. "This isn't Addison," Tony said. We need someone to get a picture of the owner, Mr. Patrick Knight. He hasn't been answering our calls. This could be why."

Addressing his detectives, he asked one of them to help get the warrants and to include this underground bunker, the house, the surveillance equipment, and grounds as well. "Once that's done, bring all the resulting material, to include videos and any data logs, to our office."

Tony left the room and began wandering around, ensuring the team was properly engaged in gathering evidence. When he encountered Donald, he looked at the glass case before him and remarked, "Looks interesting. Are these the stolen artifacts that someone called about?"

Donald turned to him and replied, "I doubt that there is anything of significance here. However, I will need to examine them in a lab to be certain."

Then Donald led Tony to an encased map that was mounted on a nearby wall. "Look at this. It is really unique. I'm guessing it was found at an archeological site and was kept for reference for continued exploration.

"Although it's displayed in a casual manner beside low-value trinkets, possibly to conceal its value, it seems likely to have been carefully protected and sealed for a reason. I am of the impression that this work was penned on ancient papyrus. I can't guess its age, but it will have to be examined by a trained specialist. It looks to me like it has been drawn on numerous times, and I guessed this because of the different inks and handwriting styles."

After hearing what Donald had just explained, Tony looked at it up close. "I would never have guessed this map was of any importance. To me it is just an old map hanging on the wall. But since you pointed them out, I see the small subtle differences. Can you tell if it's a copy or a forgery?"

Donald gently removed it from the wall, placing it on top of the glass case so he could better answer Tony's questions. As he examined it with his flashlight, he studied the variances they were able to make out before, providing additional evidence that this was likely to be an original document.

"I'm pretty certain this map is authentic and should belong to the Egyptian government, but I don't know about the other artifacts that are in the display case. In my opinion, the map is the real treasure here and is probably an important discovery. Until we know more, please don't say anything to anyone about it."

Tony was about to speak but was interrupted by some approaching detectives. "Tony, the press has showed up outside, and the coroner has not removed the body yet. Also, there is too much here to take back to the station. This bunker is huge. There are three levels of food storage, so we will have to lock it up and keep it under guard."

Tony groaned. "How many media?" he asked.

"Counting crews with cameras and photographers, about twenty people" was the answer.

"Tell them I'll talk to them shortly," he said. "In the meantime, nobody is to leak anything to the media. We need to have some answers first."

Then his cell rang, and he had a short conversation on it. "Wait," he announced to everyone. "We have our warrant signed by a judge. It covers the bunker and the manor house and all surveillance cameras, tapes, or video, and we're looking for anything that could help us learn what happened here. And we need to contact the owner as soon as we can, if he is not the victim.

"We need to make duplicates of all the notes, photographs, and surveillance tapes so we can share them with the other agencies that might get involved," he added.

The buzz of quiet conversations could be heard, as the detectives were glad to get moving on the case, especially since it meant they would finally be able to finish and get out of the closed spaces and into fresh air, where they could ditch their protective gear.

Tony walked around the bunker, mapping all the surveillance cameras and estimating the areas that were covered, as well as marking what was not covered so they could understand the activities when they viewed them back at the office. He explained to Donald what they hoped to find and how they would use the information. "When we are done down here," he said, "we will try and identify all the other cameras on the property and in the house. Hopefully we will be able to put together a complete story."

Then he expressed his curiosity about Donald's evidence. "How could you tell so quickly that the map was valuable, when it appeared to me to be a fake map from a street vendor?"

Donald smiled and replied, "The first thing that caught my attention was that it was mostly written in an ancient Hebrew dialect. No forger would attempt that, since it would be very difficult to pull off. That is also what makes it so valuable, as almost all documents we find outside of Israel, even Jewish ones, are written in the major languages of the time, such as Greek or Latin. This is a really rare find, as it is a map of ancient Alexandria that was drawn up in such a way that non-Jews couldn't read or understand it.

"I know this because we INTERPOL agents have some training in artwork and antiquities, which are the main types of items that are targeted and copied or sold throughout the world. In many instances the selling takes place through illegal organizations that have connections with underworld marketing.

"My expertise is concentrated on antiquities rather than art. That is why I was selected for this trip. In any case, this map doesn't seem to have been hidden here to sell or copy. It looks like someone stole it, or "borrowed" it just to use it for reference, possibly to help plan future archeological research.

"When I can look at it in your lab, I will know more." They tagged it as evidence, and Donald carried it out.

Tony looked up the stairs as they prepared to leave.

Donald asked, "Are you ready to see the press?"

"I can't tell them much now," said Tony, "so I will offer a press conference later, probably sometime tomorrow, and to appease the reporters, we'll get their names and give them preferential seating and answer their questions first."

As they were leaving, Tony could see that the detectives were busy getting all the information he had requested. Crossing the backyard, he saw more detectives entering the back door of the house to begin that phase of the investigation. He stopped to chat with the detective in charge to discuss the importance of the placement and view angles of the surveillance cameras.

Leaving the backyard and walking toward the driveway adjacent to the front yard, Tony approached the battery of cameras and microphones.

Eight

ADDISON AND MARIAH FLEE TO SAFETY

A soft moan alerted Addison to the fact that Mariah was awakening from her delirium, and he took her a small bowl of soup and a cup of tea. While she went through the motions of eating, he prepared her medications and set them near her with a glass of water.

"I would rather be home in my own bed," she said quietly. "I don't know what's wrong with me. When I had something like this before, I healed a lot faster."

"Just take it easy," Addison said. "You'll be fine. Is there anything I can do to make you more comfortable?"

"I'm OK," she answered. "Please, bring me up to date on everyone."

Addison updated her on what was new and reminded her that Eli and Gabriel had gone back again to ancient Alexandria.

Addison said that he had cleaning up to do and offered put something on the television that she would like to view. Waiting for her answer, Addison turned the television on and left her room.

About an hour or so later, in a keyed-up voice, Mariah called Addison to come see the news.

Addison swiftly walked to her room and looked at the television. He was shocked. A news conference was in the front yard of Patrick's house, and Tony

De La Garza, the same detective who had detained him a few days ago, was speaking. Addison turned the volume up and stood beside Mariah.

Nothing was going to be disclosed until tomorrow afternoon. Addison looked to Mariah and stated, "We have to leave now! They will discover this place fairly soon, because as soon as they identify Patrick's body and start tracking his last few days, we will be on their list of persons of interest. And they will be looking for me as a major person of interest. Not only because I live and work in his house but because I rented where we are staying right now, in his name, after he died.

"I will pack the laptops and paperwork and whatever else I think we need in Eli's car.

"We need to get to the motel and stay low. You get dressed, pack your personal things, and don't forget your medications."

They both scrambled to get everything together as quickly as possible. Addison helped Mariah to the car and then went back into the apartment-office to make sure that no important papers or information had been left behind, and he grabbed the fish bowl with the gems.

Returning to the car, Addison asked Mariah if she remembered her medications. She said yes. Starting the engine Addison pulled out of the garage and headed to the motel.

When they arrived at the motel, Addison helped Mariah into the room. He quickly unloaded the car, placing everything on the beds in the adjacent room. His first duty was putting the small fish bowl on a table and placing the treasure chest with the crystals into the fish bowl.

Addison turned the TV on. Mariah asked Addison what he was going to do and what he thought. Addison answered, "We must stay hidden and wait for Eli and Gabriel to return."

Mariah, feeling ill and in a major funk, sat twirling her wedding ring around her finger. Her eyes had a watery glaze. Seeing this, Addison tried to reassure her, saying, "Don't worry. I don't think they will look for us here. We're safe. What I need to do is set up surveillance like Sophia showed us. And we'll keep everything important packed in our backpacks ready to go."

Before an hour had passed, he had organized the food in the refrigerator and one of the closets. The table near the window had the surveillance computer set up and both go-bags ready to bug out.

After the continuous stream of activity, the sudden quiet was a shock. He had no one to talk to, he couldn't quite hear the television, and there was nothing to do. He began to reflect on what was going on, and started to try and put meaning into some of Theon's advice.

The evening news came and went without anything new—details would be provided tomorrow. He turned the television off.

"What now?" asked Mariah, after she woke up.

"Same old, same old, Mariah; we remain hidden and wait."

$$\blacktriangle \quad \blacktriangle \quad \blacktriangle$$

Tony and Donald had been working at the office since they left Patrick's mansion, and it was well past the end of the day. Tony was uneasy with what he had seen on the videos, but it gave him a better insight as to why Eli, Mariah, and Addison seemed like they did not want to divulge any information to him.

He called the lab to speak to Donald. Donald seemed excited with his research. He asked Tony if there was a place where they could speak in private about this case.

Tony suggested either his room at the hotel, where they could order room service, or they could order something to be delivered to his office, whatever his preference.

Donald said that as much as he would like to go out, he would prefer showing Tony his discoveries there in the lab. "What I have found is very intriguing, and I need to share this with you. When will you be here?"

Tony quickly answered, "I am leaving my office now, and I will be there in a few minutes."

As Tony was leaving his office, another detective was approaching him. Seeing Tony, the detective extended his hand, offering Tony a flash drive and a sheet of paper. He said, "Tony, you must see what we downloaded from within the mansion. This case appears more and more out of the ordinary as we collect and examine each new piece of evidence.

"Also some of our men found a car hidden close to the mansion. The registration shows Gabriel Reyes; his driver's license picture matches the same young man with Addison in the bunker footage. Anyway, I had his vehicle towed to the impound, and the guys examining the vehicle found that Gabriel's car had been bugged. When we compared these devices to police and FBI files, we know the bugging device used on the car towed from the Denver airport had these identical bugs."

"We'll check for fingerprints and get back with you. Thanks, Tony, the rest of us detectives appreciate the opportunity to be a part of this investigation."

Tony took the drive and thanked him, then quickly replied, "Hey, I like the way you and your cohorts are handing this part of the case. Would you object if I place you in charge of the surveillance items and all reports that go with it?"

The detective lit up. "You've got it."

Tony passed the elevator and chose to take the steps down to the lab area. Opening the door to the lab, Tony said hello to Donald. Donald stood up and motioned for Tony to join him at a light table where he had the map spread out.

Before Tony reached the desk, Donald was explaining his discoveries. "Tony, I am so excited about this find. This map has been penned by Jewish scribes because it is written in and contains references that are completed in a form of what I believe is an obscure ancient Hebrew dialect.

"This is what I think makes this map so mysterious and intriguing: the language it was penned in is Hebrew in form, but I believe some of the symbols distributed through this text are of a mathematical language that is based on an ancient Greek cryptic system. I have only seen this one other time, and I know we should turn a copy of this map over to Israeli authorities.

"Here are my questions: Why did Jews make this map so that non-Jews couldn't read or understand it?

"We have a real find here on this table. I would suggest that we copy this map and FedEx the original to Egypt. And send a copy of this map to the Israel Antiquities Authority. From there I am certain that the Israel Antiquities Authority will enjoy investigating it. I believe they will find hidden clues that we have missed because I don't understand this particular coded language, which was obviously penned to remain secret."

Tony suggested that he order dinner and that together they watched what was on the thumb drive that was downloaded off the surveillance cameras found in the bunker and mansion.

Donald agreed. Tony ordered the meal, advised the front desk that the food would be delivered, and asked that they call him at the lab when the meals arrived.

Donald and Tony started watching the surveillance data from the bunker. They saw Addison arrive with a young man, and after that the young man warned Addison that men were in the mansion. About nine minutes later, they could see the deceased person believed to be Patrick pass by the monitor. He was followed by someone in a strange costume. They appeared to be sneaking up on Addison and the young man with him.

More time passed, and they disappeared off the screen. Then, the person who was dressed in the strange costume reappeared after a few minutes, carrying a young woman who appeared to be unconscious on his shoulder.

Tony paused the flash drive and said to Donald, "When we first arrested Eli, Mariah, and Addison for the armed robbery, I had a background done on Eli, and one of the articles pulled from the social section of the newspaper showed Eli, Mariah, and their daughter, Sophia. The woman slung over the man wearing the costume looks a lot like the Daniels's daughter, Sophia.

"I wonder whether the Daniels's daughter's life was threatened, and perhaps she had already been taken hostage, and that this is why Eli, Mariah, and Addison were so tight-lipped when we had them in custody. What's really strange though is that we never saw Sophia coming into the bunker. Is it possible that she had been held prisoner here at this bunker?"

Tony restarted the playback. They saw and heard the man as he struggled to reach the top of the stairs with the young woman on his shoulder. When he did reach the top of the steps, he thrust the door open and then immediately began barking orders.

He instructed individuals to take her to the plane, drug her, and not to harm her because they needed her for leverage.

Donald, moving as close to the front of his chair as possible, sat up straight and exclaimed, "My God, what those parents must be going through and how they are suffering! I agree with you that this is a plausible explanation of why the Daniels didn't want to talk to you."

Tony remained quiet as he slowly placed the second drive into the computer so that he and Donald could view what was on this one, especially since one of the detectives helping to work the case said it was more intriguing. Tony began running the second flash drive, and he and Donald watched as a man was brought into the mansion on a stretcher.

Tony exclaimed, "That's the stranger who had the young woman on his shoulder!"

Soon a doctor arrived and treated the wounded man's injury. Tony backed the video up and tried to see what was wrong with the wounded man. He wanted to know if it was a gunshot wound.

Tony and Donald agreed that the man who carried the young woman up the stairs was struggling because of his wounds, but they couldn't agree on the nature of the injury.

Donald said, "Naturally your men will question the doctor who treated this man."

, "We haven't identified him yet, said Tony. He continued, "My men will be going in with stronger lighting so that they can check the bunker for blood trails. But I want to know who wounded him and with what."

With a voice of disbelief and excitement, Tony stated, "Perhaps there was a fight between Patrick and this man, and Patrick was killed but apparently not before Patrick wounded the stranger."

Donald added, "Although that is possible, what happened to Addison and the young man who was with him? We don't see them leaving the bunker. I wonder if there is another way out. That could explain why we never saw the young lady arrive."

Tony's cell vibrated, and he had a message that their food had arrived. "I'll be right back," he said as he left the room.

Tony returned with the food, and he and Donald watched the rest of the second flash drive and discussed following up on who the doctor was who helped the injured man. They also had to find out how Addison and the young man escaped from the bunker.

Donald remarked curiously, "Our big questions are, how did these individuals escape, who was after them, and why?"

Tony slowly spoke to Donald in a perplexed voice, "And who were those men coming in sometime later to clean the bunker?"

Donald smartly replied, "Well, Tony, I can say with certainty that they are not professionals. They missed the surveillance cameras and therefore either never knew they were being recorded or didn't care. I'm sure they have made more mistakes, and you will be able to apprehend them by following the bread crumbs."

Tony pondered. "I don't understand how they missed the cameras. They're right there, not hidden. Perhaps you are right that they didn't care if they were seen. Or, more likely, they thought we wouldn't find this place."

An uncomfortable thought occurred to Donald. "Maybe they wanted to be seen. What criminal would leave the bunker door open and not try to remove the information from the security system?"

Tony considered that for a moment, and then continued. "I wonder if they are the individuals who had a part in the false police report resulting in Eli, Mariah, and Addison being detained."

Nine

Eli and Gabriel returned from ancient Alexandria. They robed into the motel and were surprised at where they landed.

Addison explained what happened while they were gone. He told Eli that Mariah's health condition had improved very little. "She took her medicine and rested but health-wise remained where she was when you brought her home from the hospital."

Eli approached Mariah and had a short talk with her, concerned that her health was not improving. They discussed returning to the doctor for different medication.

Eli turned around to face Addison and Gabriel. Both noticed that Eli was gazing around the room; however, his eyes never settled on a person or object for long. Addison immediately recognized the issue with Eli; he was emotionally drained and feeling Mariah's pain and felt helpless.

After an awkward moment, Eli said, "While the two of you were in ancient Alexandria, I found a letter that Sophia had placed on the desk for me. It took me some time before I opened it because I knew this was the last correspondence from Rabbi Katz that I would ever receive.

"In this letter he instructs me that within the matchbox are crystals that the shomer must have for the ceremony. He also states that he couldn't find the phoenix robe, so he had an exact replica made in New York."

68

Gabriel, while mentally running through everything known about their situation, spoke up loudly, saying, "What!" which was quickly followed by Addison saying, "Please continue, Eli; we need to know what you learned."

Speaking slowly, Eli continued. "The rabbi made the trips to ancient Alexandria to secure the knowledge he needed—designs for each robe, the special material and gems necessary to complete the robes—and was in the process of collecting the needed gems for the final robe, the Phoenix robe. "He also spoke to the rabbi there about the ceremony and what he must do to bring about the downfall of this evil presence.

"Also, that business card at the bottom of the matchbox, the information on it had been written with special ink, and so I had to use lemon and heat to get the name and address of the seamstress who made the robes for Rabbi Katz.

"He made sure the card looked like the bottom of the matchbox so that no one would think anything of it.

"The seamstress apparently has the Phoenix robe, which is an absolute necessity for the success of our mission. We need to go get that robe for the shomer before you two leave to Alexandria to join Shamar and Sophia."

Addison was quick to reply to Eli and Gabriel. "Gabriel, you must go to New York and get the robe. After securing the robe, come straight back here to us at the motel."

Addison moved quickly to the computer and made the reservation. He hit print and promptly had the ticket for Gabriel. Without a delay, Addison went to the drawer and pulled out some money. As he handed the money to Gabriel, he stated, "The ticket is a one-way because, as I mentioned earlier, I believe you can robe back here. Just read the traveling prayer." He copied the prayer onto a piece of paper and gave it to Gabriel.

Eli asked, "Addison, where are you getting all this seemingly endless money?"

Addison smiled and replied, "When Edward thought he might be in trouble because of the items he accidently brought back from Alexandria, he began putting money away in various-sized boxes, and he placed these boxes throughout the bunker.

"Also, he opened a secret account that he and I were both on just in case I needed to get the money for him. I just helped myself to some of it so that we could do things without financial worries and without banks or authorities knowing how much we were spending or where we were spending it. It is an offshore account that has not been used for some time. And generally this bank keeps client information confidential.

Addison continued. "Oh, and I used this special bank account that Edward set up for us to purchase the airline ticket."

Gabriel looked at the printed ticked and said that he needed to hurry and that he would keep in touch via the cell phone. "Addison, you need to drop me off at the airport. I don't have time to park."

Mariah had slowly and quietly walked into the living room, and she asked Addison if her health condition was the same as Edward's. This was awkward. Addison knew he must be indirect in order not to panic her. He told her that her illness and Edward's were similar but different. "Edward continued to slide down in health, while you are holding steady."

Turning to Eli, Addison carried on his thoughts. "Eli will take you to the doctor because I think he feels the same as I, and that is that you need a different prescription."

Eli moved toward Mariah to help her onto the couch. Mariah's mind flashed with memories of Edward's last days, and she had images of her uncertain future, given her present health condition. She remained very silent.

Addison and Eli understood that she was struggling with her physical condition, so Eli went to the phone and called the family doctor and explained the situation and asked for medical advice for Mariah. The doctor's answering service asked that Eli bring her in for an examination, suggesting that they might require a different medication.

Eli and Mariah left for the hospital to meet their doctor, and Addison took Sophia's car to get Gabriel to the airport.

The drive to the hospital was uneventful. No one appeared to be following them, and they didn't see any suspicious characters as they entered the clinic. After a short visit, a new prescription for Mariah had been written, and they went to the pharmacy to fill the prescription. They had been waiting about ten minutes when a well-dressed elder gentleman entered the room, looked around, and walked directly to where they sat.

The stranger stopped in front of Eli and Mariah, tipped his hat, and began speaking. "You don't know me," he said, "but I know who you are. We had a mutual friend, Rabbi Katz. Pity what happened to him, kind of sudden and unexpected."

Mariah clutched Eli's hand out of concern and sheer fear.

Eli, likewise, was taken aback. He paled, and squeezed Mariah's hand anxiously. He quickly asked, "Who are you?"

The stranger smiled a grandfatherly smile and ignored Eli's question. "You both seem like nice people. Rabbi Katz was as well. It's a shame he chose to meddle in things that were none of his business.

"It appears that some misinformed people influenced the rabbi's decision to seek and collect several unusual stones and artifacts to prevent a number of imagined future catastrophes."

There was a brief pause, and with a slower delivery, the elderly gentleman continued. "The rabbi had been given a wrong impression of these artifacts. I hope he hasn't persuaded you to take up his quest because I am aware that the rabbi was carrying out his work based on inaccurate information. He thought he was helping, but if successful he could have prevented the greatest boon to humankind in history.

"The rabbi was correct that new leadership is being brought forward to revitalize hope to all humankind. This new leadership has been anticipated for centuries.

"This leader will bring greatness to humankind. He will help humans achieve their full potential, and no more will they be weak and struggling. Please consider what I have shared with you, and make the correct decision. I am always available and willing to help both of you. Just seek me."

The elder gentleman took a small step backward, bowed, and tipped his hat. Turning slowly he walked away.

An incredulous stare was on both of their faces as Eli and Mariah remained silent and shocked at what they had just been told. They watched as the elderly man exited down the hallway and then disappeared from sight.

After a long pause, Eli turned to Mariah and asked, "What just happened? Who was that person, and how did he find us and why did he know of the rabbi's quest?" And then, "Surely the rabbi wasn't inadvertently trying to prevent the coming of the Messiah! I don't think the Messiah would tolerate kidnapping and murder."

Both remained in a dazed state, saying nothing, but each silently contemplated what had transpired.

Mariah grabbed Eli by the hand and, facing him, stated, "We can't go to the car or our motel. With terror in her voice, she continued. "Look." She pointed to the parking lot. "The authorities have surrounded our car, and I don't trust the old man who just spoke with us. We need a plan."

Eli squeezed her hand and verbally confirmed that he too had the same thought. Both sat for a while, deep in thought, thinking of alternatives.

Eli asked her if she had any ideas. Mariah replied, "I can't think of anything." After a moment Mariah said, "Eli, I'm still wearing the robe. You could say the prayer again, and we're out of here."

Eli replied, "That's what I love about you. Always a level head." He guided her to a secluded corner, took her into his arms, and recited the traveling prayer.

When they arrived at the motel, Eli and Mariah discussed what had happened at the hospital.

Addison had just arrived back from the airport. He listened as Eli explained what had transpired at the hospital pharmacy. Addison was shocked at the information the elderly man at the pharmacy presented. Addison's main questions during this discussion were, "How did this man know you? And know where you were? And how did he know so much about the rabbi?"

Addison then volunteered to go get Mariah's prescription. He would use Sophia's car. Quickly he recommended that they pack everything that was necessary and get ready for a speedy getaway.

Addison returned and together the three of them began updating their plans for modern-day Alexandria to include new code words and meeting places.

Eli spoke of his concern for Mariah and her traveling. The dialogue between the three became heated as Addison presented his increased concern for their success in Alexandria.

Realizing that this discussion was adding to Mariah's distress, Eli opened the new medication and gave her the appropriate dose. He then tucked her into bed and rejoined Addison in the living room.

Both men were silent for a few moments, and then Eli reengaged the discussion about what they should do now. The encounter at the pharmacy obviously rattled Eli, and he wanted to know how and where they should proceed to accomplish their tasks.

After numerous ideas they couldn't agree on a solution. Addison finally stated that they should cross that bridge when they came to it and that for now they needed to do what was necessary as each issue arose.

Essentially, they would be playing it by the moment and using extreme caution. Addison told Eli that he would inform the others of the new danger that had presented itself in the form of the stranger.

Hours passed, and Eli received a text from Gabriel. "Have phoenix robe. Returning home." Eli texted back, "Message received."

Many hours passed, and Gabriel had not robed in or texted. Eli and Addison began verbalizing their concern for Gabriel. Addison expressed uncertainty over letting Gabriel go alone to New York and pulled his cell phone out to call the seamstress, asking her if Gabriel was still there. "Oh, no," she replied. "He left several hours ago. If he got delayed, his friend probably caught up with him, and he probably lost track of time visiting with him. His friend had just arrived at my shop moments after Gabriel left."

Addison thanked the seamstress and hung up. With a tinge of fright in his voice, Addison quietly informed Eli of what the seamstress said. "How could anybody know he was there? We told no one."

Eli was concerned with Addison's report. Both heard Mariah gasp, and they realized she had silently entered the living room. Each also knew that she had overheard their discussion.

Mariah asked what they should do. Addison paused before answering and then said, "We wait to hear from him. If evil has captured him, someone would have robed in by now, so I think it is something else and that Gabriel will contact us as soon as he is able."

Each secretly wondered whether the elderly man had something to do with Gabriel's delay.

▲ ▲ ▲

Gabriel was surprised to awaken in ancient Alexandria; it was not the motel as he had planned. He looked around quickly to see if the man who was following him from the seamstress's shop had also landed nearby. He had not. Fortunately no one had noticed him asleep in the square.

Gabriel was shocked to realize that he was in ancient Alexandria, and he could hear the loud noise of an angry crowd nearby. "This is really bad," he said to himself, and his muscles tightened for action as he prepared for the worst.

Not wanting to lose the robe, Gabriel secured the drawstring sack to his belt.

Slowly approaching the street, Gabriel was met by a large mob of zealots. "There's one of them now!" he heard, as they all rushed to attack him. As much as he tried, he was unable to avoid capture; there were too many people in the mob, and he was overwhelmed.

The men thrust Gabriel over their shoulders and carried him to their leaders. After a hasty trial, Gabriel was found guilty of apostasy. They then turned their attention to the mob and asked them how they wanted Gabriel executed.

The crowd's shouts of "Burn him alive! Burn him alive!" echoed throughout the area as the zealot's leader stood silent, watching Gabriel's reaction.

The leader walked over to Gabriel and placed his face as close as possible to Gabriel's, as though looking into his soul to see the evil. He then raised his arm and shouted back to the crowd, "Let's burn him alive!"

The crowd roared in agreement with the decision, and Gabriel was quickly shuffled around and tied to a pole. The crowd dragged Gabriel through town to a prepared area for his execution. During the short trip through the streets, bystanders threw whatever they had in their hands at Gabriel and shouted obscenities.

After they reached their destination, the pole holding Gabriel was dropped into place, and men piled stones around it to hold it up. Others were gathering wood, sticks, and straw and placing them around Gabriel's feet.

Gabriel tried to get out of the ropes holding him to the pole, but they were securely strapped to his arms and legs. Keeping his composure Gabriel began thinking of how to escape. Looking around he thought it odd that there were no soldiers patrolling the streets. Realizing that no one would come to rescue him, he wondered what had gone wrong with the transportation prayer.

They lit the tinder at his feet, and as the smoke overcame him, he couldn't remember any of the transportation prayers. As he began to lose consciousness, an old shepherd man in robes appeared through the smoky billows and whispered some words into his ear, which he promptly repeated. Then to his amazement, he found himself waking up on the ground, looking up at a strange man in modern dress.

The stranger shouted, "There you are, and my goodness are you late! We need to get started with the ceremony as soon as possible. Do you have the artifacts? Where is Rabbi Katz?"

Gabriel was frightened that this stranger wasn't shocked and even seemed to expect him. With his hands now free from the bindings, Gabriel grabbed the prayer from his pocket and read it out loud. He heard the man shout, "No!" as he felt the spinning begin.

Within moments he was transported again. With a noticeable thud, he landed in darkness; the only light was from someone's flashlight in the short distance in front of him.

Gabriel soon realized the owner of the light was Shamar, and Sophia was beside him. Shamar was clearly shocked to see Gabriel but quickly motioned for Gabriel to be quiet by placing his finger across his lips. Gabriel remained silent and listened.

Shamar could hear men carrying on a dialogue on the other side of the wall. Their conversation escalated into a heated argument as their voices were filled with surprise and anger that their prey had escaped their capture and they could find no visible exit. It was especially obvious that the man who seemed to be in charge was stymied. The tone in his voice had increased with a sense of desperation.

Cursing in the next room permeated the wall and grew in volume into a loud diatribe. "There is no place they could have gone!" the voice shouted to the others. Even louder, the voice demanded, "There were no side tunnels and no exits. Shamar and Sophie could not have just disappeared. There have to be hidden exits. Find them!"

After a long wait, they heard the men leaving.

Shamar turned toward Sophia and Gabriel, and moving his face close to theirs, he quietly asked them to remain silent until they were certain that the men on the other side were actually gone.

Several minutes had passed, and hearing nothing from the other side of the wall, Shamar whispered to Gabriel, "What are you doing here?"

Softly Gabriel answered, "You won't believe what just happened to me. A man was following me in New York, and I tried to dodge him by going through alleys and zigzagging down streets, but I realized that I couldn't get away.

"But I said the wrong prayer and landed in ancient Alexandria, where they tried to roast me like a witch. So to get away, I said the prayer again, and I landed next to a man who said I was late and that we needed to hurry for the ceremony, and something about Rabbi Katz. So, I grabbed my prayer from my pocket and read the correct prayer, and this time I came here, to you and Sophia. I am glad to be with both of you."

Shamar and Sophia looked surprised at what he said. Shamar quietly said, "We need to talk about all that, especially the man who said you were late and asked about Rabbi Katz and the ceremony, but later. Our immediate need is to find our way out of wherever we are and get back on track.

There was a very short pause, and Shamar continued. "We're here in modern Alexandria, and we found the tunnel. While conducting our investigation of Mariah's map, we heard men approaching us from within the tunnel. One of them spoke in a low voice, but the echo from the small tunnel reverberated what he said, and he reminded whoever was accompanying him that they were instructed to take us alive—and he knew our names!"

Vincent's plane had landed, and the head of his security team said that there were men at the bottom of the stairs and that they ordered him and the rest of the team off the plane. However they had requested that Vincent remain on the plane for further instructions.

Vincent thanked the guard and gave orders to the men to break up into two men per group and for each group to separate out all over Alexandria and look for Shamar and Sophia.

He added that they were to have no interactions with anybody they're shadowing, just to report where they are and what they are doing. He waved his hand, gesturing for the men to be on their way.

Shortly after the group's departure, four individuals boarded Vincent's plane. Vincent recognized three of the men and knew this was more than a casual visit.

The person in charge of the group stepped forward and said to Vincent that he was instructed to inform him that Senka had a new caretaker and purpose.

The leader of the group looked at Vincent, for his reaction about Senka. After a moment, he continued by pointing to a young man standing at his side and quickly explaining to Vincent, "This is Robert, a new member of your team. He has been briefed and given his specific orders and what is expected of him. As for your duties, Vincent, the phantom wants the watchman and the crystals that the he carries with him. Your main objective is to stop him. And by the way, the people we are bugging refer to him as 'the shomer.'"

The messenger and the two who accompanied him disappeared, leaving only Robert standing close to Vincent.

Tony and Donald met in Tony's office to prepare their strategies before notifying the FBI. After making sure that he had copies of all flash drives and the map, Tony called the local FBI office and explained the reason for the call was that they had a possible kidnapping on videotape and that they wanted to discuss the case with them.

There was silence in the room as Tony listened. Then Tony spoke in a more forceful voice. "You should know that a vehicle we found near the scene of this murder-kidnapping investigation has the same bugging equipment on it as the car you took from Denver International a few days ago. We suspect that these two cases are connected.

"And INTERPOL has sent an agent from England, a Mr. Donald Wellington, to assist, as the case involves possible stolen artifacts from Egypt."

Within moments, Tony hung up the phone and told Donald about the call. "The FBI is sending an agent over immediately to talk to us and to get all the information we have."

Tony then turned to Donald and asked, "Have you sent the original map to Egypt yet? If you haven't I would suggest giving it to one of my men so he can make copies and take it to FedEx now."

Donald smiled and said, "No, it has not yet been sent. Yes, it is packaged and ready to be shipped, and I have already made copies for my office, which are also ready to be mailed.

"I took the liberty of making copies for you too, which are on my desk in the lab. I would appreciate it if you would have your detectives mail both of my packages before the FBI gets here, please.

"And you should know that I sent a photo of the map to Israel too, via my cell phone. As soon as Israel responds, I'll let you know. I also informed the Israel authorities that I am in the process of FedExing the original map to Egyptian authorities and that it should be in the mail today."

Ten

THE SHOMER

S hamar began explaining to Gabriel that when he and Sophia were exploring the recently excavated tunnels under the temple, they heard voices and
immediately teleported and surprisingly found themselves just on the other
side of the wall from the area they had been exploring. Once they reached
this side of the wall, they could hear the men enter the area that they had just
abandoned. "And then you came!" Shamar added.

"We need to hurry," Sophia said quietly. "We have to figure out where we
are and find a way out."

They continued down this new tunnel, and Shamar brought Gabriel up
to date on what he and Sophia had done since their arrival in modern-day
Alexandria. After a pause, he added, "I don't understand how those men knew
our names and where to find us! It doesn't make sense."

"I didn't see anyone following us," Sophie answered. "I'm scared."

Gabriel thought for a moment. "They must have hidden really well when
they followed you." After a pause he added, "I need to tell you what we did
back in old Alexandria," and, as they continued down the tunnel, he proceeded to tell them all that he, Addison, and Eli had accomplished in ancient
Alexandria. He added that the situation in ancient Alexandria had deterio-
rated so badly that Quintus, Avitus, and their men were preparing to leave.

"Good job," said Shamar. "We need to be careful, and as soon as we get out of here, we have to warn the others."

Commenting on the tunnel, Shamar compared the similarity of the first tunnel and this one. Sophia remarked that the whole area seemed a mirror image, except for the thick cobwebs and total lack of restoration.

They finally reached an archway at the end of the tunnel that opened into darkness. Shamar remembered the small bridge and the two deep pits flanking it that were at the other tunnel entrance and hesitated to move forward.

Shamar and Gabriel inched ahead slowly, with Sophia following behind them. Their flashlights illuminated very little before them, and Gabriel remarked that the echo of their footsteps had changed, indicating that they had entered a more confined area.

Sophia focused her flashlight on a wall just to the left of the archway, remarking that the mirror image aspect seemed to change at this point. The narrow bridge and deep pits apparently were not replicated here.

Shamar and Gabriel looked at where her flashlight was pointing, and they too shone theirs toward the same spot. Shinning their lights down the whole left side, they saw where this wall was intersected by another, and they could see they had entered another room.

Shamar and Gabriel began following the wall to see where it led. Sophia, at the rear, occasionally turned her flashlight upward to see if there was a ceiling, stairway, ladder, or anything that could help them find their way out.

Sophia remarked that they seemed to be in a small rectangular room. Shamar agreed and added that there must be a way out; they just needed to find it.

The three shone their flashlights up on the ceiling in an organized effort to see if there was a way out that might be above them.

"Look," said Gabriel, pointing to a recess in the ceiling. "That looks kind of like part of a chimney, and it seems to have a shelf in the side. In fact, he added, "I think I see rope or something up there."

"I see it too," responded Shamar. "You might be right; it could be a rope." He squinted, trying to make out the dusty shape in the ceiling.

Shamar stood on Gabriel's shoulders, and after numerous tries he snagged a piece of the rope. Soon Gabriel felt the weight of Shamar's body release from his shoulders, and the two of them watched as Shamar pulled himself up the rope with his flashlight in his mouth to free up both hands, climbing up through the ceiling.

Shamar noticed that there was a latch just to the right of the where the rope was secured. He moved the latch to open what appeared to be a trap door in the ceiling. As he cautiously opened the door, several pounds of accumulated sand and pebbles cascaded down upon them, and then after the dust cleared, he saw Pompey's Pillar through a small opening, a short distance from him. Concentrating for a moment to get his bearings, he realized that they were inside the lion statue near the pillar.

Shamar returned his attention to the rope, dropping the loose end to the floor beside Sophia and Gabriel. It took some time, but by helping each other and being cautious to remain unseen, they eventually crawled out of the base of the lion statue. Gabriel was the last to exit and closed the trap door. All three now scrambled to the street below and hurried to the café where Shamar and Sophia had eaten where they discussed what to do next over strong, gritty coffee.

Sophia texted Addison and told him that Gabriel was with them, and they would join him shortly so they could all meet at the place where Avitus and two of his men helped Shamar retrieve the scroll.

▲ ▲ ▲

The phantom received a new text: "We just found Sophia, Shamar, and Gabriel near the pillar. They just texted Addison stating that they would be joining him soon. Also we have a new name, Avitus, and perhaps someone can do research to gather what information we need about him. Plans are to meet where Avitus found the Scroll of Knowledge."

The phantom immediately answered, "Wonderful. Stay out of sight and follow them, keeping me informed."

The guard turned to his partner and said, "Our new assignment is to follow them quietly." That was the last thing he ever said, as he felt the sharp pain of a knife entering his abdomen. The attack was unanticipated; however, the guard instinctively retaliated, wrestling with the other guard, and in the struggle he successfully grabbed the knife and returned a blow. As his vision faded, he realized his life was over, but he had the satisfaction of knowing he had inflicted a mortal wound on his attacker.

▲ ▲ ▲

Sophia, Shamar, and Gabriel made their way to the Temple of Canopus. Gabriel robed to Denver to get Addison. Hours went by before Gabriel and Addison arrived at the Temple of Canopus. Addison gave Sophia and Shamar each a big hug and then remarked that he was glad that they were together and safe.

A grimace formed on Addison's face as he stated that he needed to bring them up to date on what had taken place in Denver, but first he wanted to know what Shamar and Sophia's investigations had turned up.

Shamar and Sophia explained that a historical society was conducting a renovation right where they needed to explore. They did find the secret room and tunnel that Mariah and Eli spoke of, and while examining these specific areas they had to robe to safety because someone had followed them into the tunnel. They told him the shocking fact that the people who had followed them down the tunnel knew precisely who they were and where to find them!

With a surprised voice, he asked, "Are you sure? How is that possible?" he added rhetorically. A sudden chill ran down his spine as he realized the evil ones were a lot closer to being able to capture them than anyone had anticipated.

To avoid showing his alarm, he turned gradually to face Gabriel and changed the subject. "We were all worried about you when you didn't return from the seamstress as expected. What happened? Why didn't you come back?" he asked.

Gabriel explained that he was certain he was being followed when he left the seamstress shop in New York, so he ducked into an alley and said the prayer to escape. He stated that he must have made a mistake when reciting the prayer because he ended up in ancient Alexandria instead of modern-day Alexandria. He explained where he landed and what happened. He then explained a chance encounter with someone speaking about the ceremony and Rabbi Katz when he tried to return.

"That's great!" Addison said. "That's probably the shomer. Where was he?"

"I don't know," Gabriel replied. "I was still afraid from my experience with the mob, and I transported out of there immediately."

Restraining an impulse to roll his eyes, Addison asked, "Do you remember which prayer got you to him?"

"No," answered Gabriel. "While I was in the fire, some old shepherd guy in a robe appeared and told me the words, and I don't remember what they were."

"I wish you could remember; however, I'm not surprised the mob wanted to execute you. But I'm glad that it seems that Avitus, Quintus, and their men had already departed Alexandria safely."

Addison shifted his questions to learn about Shamar and Sophia's experiences. After their answers he told everyone of the encounter Eli and Mariah had with the old man at the hospital and that Eli's car had been taken by the authorities.

At this point Addison paused for a moment, reflecting on the similarity in the two situations. The stranger who met Eli and Mariah at the hospital knew where to find them, and he knew their names. And now in this similar incident, strangers knew where to find Sophia and Shamar, and knew who they were. *It's as though they have tracking devices on everyone.*

Turning to Sophia he told her that her parents should be there shortly. "I forwarded your text to them so that they will know where to meet us."

Sophia looked at her watch and suggested that they go back to a nearby park and get some breakfast from one of the vendors.

Addison agreed and said that he would like a light meal too, to go with their conversation, of course.

Addison stopped and turned to Shamar saying, "Shamar, I got the wax that you requested." Reaching into his pocket, he handed him the wax-covered box. Shamar took it and thanked him.

The four left the cave and headed toward the Alexandria Citadel. The walk would take about thirty to forty minutes.

When they had almost reached the Citadel, Gabriel stopped, turned to Shamar, and quietly said, "Would you all listen to me and stop walking toward the vendors?" Everyone halted and gave their attention to Gabriel.

Gabriel told everyone not to look but some man appeared to be following them. Shamar took Sophia's hand and suggested that they go to the shaved ice kiosk, which stayed open all hours of the day and night for tourists, and for Gabriel to keep an eye out to see if this stranger would continue following them. Everyone agreed.

Gabriel observed that the man was still following them but with more distance between him and the group. Apparently the stranger suspected they might have seen him. Gabriel knew that he must do something before they lost the opportunity to speak to this individual. He weighed that against the potential danger—they might have to run.

Reaching the kiosk, they watched as the proprietor and his wife were replenishing the syrups and adding ice to the machine. Sophia placed the order for everyone.

While the man was preparing their shaved ice, Addison motioned for everyone to follow him and join him at a bench. Away from the earshot of others, Addison explained to the group that the police had found Patrick's body and begun an investigation. He said that he was glad that Sophia had gotten the motel because it gave them a place to retreat to.

Gabriel mentioned that the man who had been following them was now just watching them. Before anyone could react, Gabriel decided to confront the man directly, and he bolted to the man and immediately asked the stranger why he was following them.

The man acknowledged that he was following them because he was looking for some colleagues or associates of his good friend Rabbi Katz, and their appearance matched the description of those whom he was seeking.

Addison, Shamar, and Sophia had followed behind Gabriel and heard the conversation. All were taken aback. Addison stepped forward and asked the man to please have a seat at a nearby bench with them and explain himself to all of them at once.

At the bench, their discussion involved more questions and answers than a proper conversation, on both sides. The stranger claimed to be the shomer, said that Rabbi Katz contacted him for assistance with a ceremony, and that he was concerned because he hadn't heard from the rabbi since their last meeting. The stranger also wished to know if they had recovered all the artifacts required for the ceremony.

Addison snapped at the stranger over the last question. "Do you think it wise to discuss in public that which is so sacred and secret! Do you realize people are trying to kill us over this?"

The shomer seemed unconcerned with Addison's sharp rebuke but pleased that Addison showed awareness and didn't deny possession of the artifacts.

The shomer asked if Addison could gather the items and meet him at the pillar so that the ceremony could be performed.

While the others were exchanging small talk with the shomer, Shamar texted Eli, "We found the shomer."

The shomer stated, "The sooner we complete this mission, the quicker we will be out of danger, and then all of us can return to a normal life."

Sophia hastily made a comment to the shomer, "Rabbi Katz would be so proud of all of us."

The shomer looked stunned with Sophia's comment and responded, "What do you mean *would* be proud of us?"

Addison quickly interjected, "The rabbi died suddenly several days ago."

The shomer looked shocked at learning of the rabbi's death and said, "May God bless his soul," and made the sign of the cross on his chest. Gabriel, being a good Catholic, did the same.

Sophia was stunned but hid her fear. She didn't want the shomer to recognize her sudden distress, so she took in a deep breath and threw herself into Shamar's arms and began crying on his shoulder. Shamar, surprised by Sophia's behavior instantly held her tightly and began gently rocking her as she wept.

Addison realized that he was not the only one to comprehend the situation, so he turned to the shomer and replied to him that she was still overcome with grief by the rabbi's sudden death.

Addison looked to the shomer and requested they meet with him at the pillar tomorrow night at nine thirty. "We need time to gather all the sacred items required for the ceremony," he said.

The shomer smiled as he shook Addison's hand and agreed to the time and place. Addison immediately looked to Shamar and Sophia and said, "We must leave now and gather that which is necessary."

Returning his attention to the shomer, Addison stated in a forthright manner, "Your life is in grave danger just being seen with us. You must leave now. Good day."

The four turned and started walking away, Sophia clinging to Shamar's waist and he hers. She thanked him for being so understanding. Shamar handed her his paper napkin so she could wipe her tears.

Gabriel looked back and didn't see the shomer at all. He then commented on how nice the shomer was and how fortunate it was they met him.

Shamar commented, "That was close."

Sophia interjected in a shocked and frightened voice, "How did he find us?"

Addison calmly added, "And how did he know so much? We need to change our plans immediately. There are some stone benches ahead that we can sit at and plan our next steps."

"Hey, Americans!" someone called out. "Your shaved ice is ready." They had forgotten it. Shamar returned to the stand and paid the man, then followed the group toward the benches, with syrup dripping down his fingers.

Puzzled, Gabriel had been unable to understand their conversation. With bewilderment in his voice, he asked Addison, "What's going on? What are the three of you talking about?

Just then, the ground began to shake, bushes waved back and forth, and people in the kiosks looked frightened. Addison immediately looked to the water in the bay to see if the water was affected by the earth's movement. It was. Small boats, hitched to the pier, were bobbing up and down, and some almost tipped over from the strong movement of the water.

Addison asked, "Did anyone else feel that? That was an earthquake!"

Shamar answered, "Yes. Sophia and I felt a similar movement while we were in the tunnel exploring. I thought it was a large truck or equipment that the workers were using during their restoration work."

They slowed their pace, and Addison, to keep anyone who might be watching from becoming suspicious, helped Shamar pass out the treats while he spoke in a low voice, finally answering Gabriel's question, "Gabriel, our Jewish shomer seems to be Catholic. Jews do not make the sign of the cross."

Gabriel's face flushed, and he said, "I'm glad the rest of you caught his mistake. I'll keep an eye out to see if we're being followed by any of his acquaintances."

Addison looked around and led the four toward an area where a stone seat was available for all of them to sit and discuss what to do.

Just before he reached the stone seat, a beggar limped in front of Addison, forcing him to stop. The beggar quickly but quietly asked, "Can you donate something for a poor man?" Then he continued in a much lower voice. "Perhaps a flask or a robe or a scroll?"

Swiftly the beggar gestured by placing his fingers to his lips for them to be quiet. Everyone was surprised and momentarily speechless from the beggar's words and gesturing.

Before anyone could say anything, the beggar flashed his cell phone for everyone to see. Addison was stunned to read the text message that Shamar had just sent to Eli. Concentrating on the beggar's features, Addison, in a surprised, low voice whispered, "Sago!"

Sophia thought she recognized something familiar about this beggar's voice and now she saw a face that resembled the man she had seen on the security monitors during her escape.

Sago promptly whispered, "Don't say my name because I have a price on my head, but before I die, I want to help you and your friends.

"Your phones are bugged, all of your phones," he whispered. "The master bug was placed in Eli's phone while he was at the hospital with Mariah, and that is how they know where you are. They also know everything you say when you call or text each other, and most important, they know your exact location.

"Those seeking your ultimate destruction have a state-of-the-art GPS system tracking each of you through your phones as well as all communication with each other, and everyone who has communicated with Eli's number. Get rid of the phones because they will be able to track and kill you one by one or as a group. There is a bounty on each of you, as well as the robes, flasks, and scrolls, and the amount of money offered is very high."

There were a few seconds of stunned silence, and then Sophia moved toward Sago to speak with him, but before a single word could cross her lips, Sago quickly told her, "I instructed my men to allow you to escape but to make it look like they tried to capture you. I never wanted to harm any of Addison's friends, and it would have endangered lives if I tried to warn Addison."

Sophia stopped and stared. The whisper that crossed her lips was directed to Sago, "Why should I believe you?"

Sago's voice lacked the power to complete his thought. His speech was broken or trailing off while his lips moved. He grabbed the sleeve of his shirt and squeezed it hard. Then he extended his hand toward Addison.

Addison slid Sago some coins as he put his hand forward for a donation. He thanked Sago for his help. Sago paused for just a moment, taking in every moment of this experience, and looked at the coins and then back to Addison, whispering, "You're welcome, my dear brother." Tears filled Sago's eyes as he gave what he knew would be his final glance into Addison's face.

Addison wanted to hug him, but Sago turned too quickly, bumping into Gabriel, and then in a split second, he was gone.

Addison was touched that Sago had finally done the right thing for the right reason, and he realized that when Sago said there was a price on his head, he meant it literally. Surprised at what had just taken place, he watched as Sago limped away from them. He was unsure what to say as he watched Sago struggle to leave them.

Addison realized that Sago was paying the ultimate price to help him and his friends survive. Tears welled up in Addison's eyes as he realized Sago was staggering as he walked away from them.

Addison, along with the others, saw that the hair on Sophia's arms had risen, her face was flushed with anger, and Addison knew she was extremely upset. He also saw that Sophia's fake tears were now real tears, tears of anger and disbelief directed at him.

In a low and angry but controlled voice, Sophia said, "Addison, you know this man! This is the man who kidnapped me and held me hostage. To what extent do you know him, and how did he know where we are?"

Gabriel went in closer to Addison, waiting for his answers, prepared to protect him from Sophia, while Shamar remained at her side.

"Yes," replied Addison. "I'll tell you everything as soon as we get rid of these phones. Please be cautious of what you say and whose name you use."

Addison saw the shock, disbelief, and agitation that Shamar and Sophia manifested through their facial expressions, and for the first time, he felt unsafe among his friends.

Pulling back, Shamar and Sophia retreated a small distance from Addison. Addison's first thought was that they were remaining silent to keep from giving away information. But then he realized that they now had doubts about him and his loyalty.

Shamar turned from Addison as he directed a remark to Gabriel and Sophia, "Our run-in with that man has changed things considerably; however, I want to hear what Addison has to say before we rush to any judgment."

"Do you think we can trust Addison?" Sophia whispered to Shamar.

There was a long pause before Shamar answered. "I think we can. If that was Sago, and I'm positive from your reaction and Addison's that it was, then Sago has risked his life just to warn us."

Gabriel moved closer to Sophia, gave her a small hug, and said, "I'm positive Sago used his cell phone to find us and warn us of danger. And I believe that the fake shomer also used a similar cell phone to find us.

"Moreover, that is why the shomer knew so much about what we were doing; the fake shomer and Sago had been listening in to our conversations, Sago to protect us and the 'shomer' to deceive us."

There was a short break, and Shamar added, "We need to hear what Addison has to say. Addison didn't betray us; the bugged cell phones did.

However, Addison has known about Sago because of his relationship with him, and that is what I want to understand, the relationship and why he kept it secret."

Gabriel softly interjected, "I agree with Shamar; however, Addison was truly surprised when he saw Sago, and I refuse to believe that Addison is a member of the dark side. I have the same opinion as Shamar that we need to listen to Addison first and go from there. And, when Sago was leaving, he didn't rush off but walked away with difficulty. I think he has already been critically injured and was trying to hide his wound."

It looked to Shamar as if Sophia was going to speak, but she said nothing. Looking into Shamar's eyes, Sophia gently squeezed his hand and, with a shaking, low voice, said, "I need a minute alone." She walked a short distance from him to a different stone bench.

Gabriel and Shamar watched her as she began moving away from them. She was just a few steps away, and Shamar quickly moved to her side. Taking her into his arms, he said, "We will get through this together. These last few hours have been rough for you, for all of us, but I am here to help, and so is Gabriel."

Sophia placed her head on his chest and softly began to cry. As he held her, Shamar wondered if she was at a breaking point. He was also very concerned about the new turn of events and had a greater worry for everyone's safety. Gradually Shamar's thoughts focused on Eli and Mariah. *Where are they? Are they all right?* Then he remembered that Addison was the last to have contact with them. *Should I be worried that Addison is the only one who knows how they are doing?*

"Everyone wait here," Gabriel announced, "while I run an errand," and he began collecting their cell phones. He was going to dispose of the phones, perhaps by spreading them throughout a hotel.

Everyone agreed, but Addison grabbed at Gabriel's arm and asked to go with him. "I need to send a telegram to Eli and Mariah telling them of the latest danger."

Addison and Gabriel left together, and Sophia and Shamar waited for them near the stone benches.

Gabriel placed phones in two different hotel lobbies. While at the last hotel, Addison sent a Western Union message to Eli and Mariah.

Eleven

When Eli awakened he saw an envelope had been pushed under the motel door. He walked to the door, grasped the envelope, and opened it. It was a Western Union message addressed to him. Puzzled that he would even receive a telegram, he opened it and was shocked at its message.

Eli quickly reread it, this time examining the message to calculate how much time had elapsed and to look for the agreed upon codes to ensure the identity of the person who sent the message. *So that is how the old man found us! I wonder if he knows about this motel.*

Without delay he glanced at his security computer to see if they were being watched. He considered the imminent danger that he and Mariah were in and decided that they had to flee immediately. Wanting Mariah to get as much rest as possible, Eli dressed and packed as much as possible before he awakened her.

Having successfully stashed their belongings in the car, Eli draped Mariah's clothing over the back of the chair and inspected the room for anything that he might have missed. He then gently awakened Mariah and told her that he was taking her out for a special breakfast.

Having received a sluggish response from Mariah, Eli asked her how she felt. Mariah responded that she was feeling better but had a terrible headache.

Tenderly, she held Eli's hand and reassured him that it was probably because of the change in medications.

Eli took her into his arms and kissed her. He then stated that she should get dressed and that after breakfast they must make new decisions.

Mariah removed her nightgown slowly and got into the clothing that Eli had placed on the chair for her. She was in such a fog that she didn't notice that their belongings were no longer in the room. When she was dressed, Eli grabbed her nightgown and extended his arm so that he could escort her to the car.

He started the engine, looked over at Mariah, slowly pulled away from the motel, and then headed down the road, contemplating a quiet place to have breakfast as he drove toward the airport.

Choosing a gas station near the airport, Eli stopped to fill up the car, and he dumped the cell phones into the container of windshield washer fluid while waiting for the tank to fill.

After filling the car, Eli returned to the driver's seat and showed Mariah the telegram from Addison and told her that he had just dumped both of their phones into the windshield wiper container. "No!" she exclaimed. "How do we communicate with them?"

"We'll get by," he responded. "Addison was able to send us this warning, so I believe they are all aware of the danger and have taken the appropriate steps. Perhaps you and I could discuss a new plan."

Mariah had trouble concentrating. Her headache bothered her greatly, and she was preoccupied with worrying about Sophia and the others' safety. She wanted to speak but couldn't organize her thoughts.

Distressed from witnessing her misery, Eli choked a little as he attempted to comfort her with reassurance that he knew everyone would be all right.

She knew he didn't know that; he just wanted to keep her from worrying.

He finally saw a restaurant that they liked and pulled in to have breakfast. The waitress, observing their melancholy, addressed them cheerfully and tried to lift their spirits with pleasant chatter, but to no avail. They solemnly ordered their food and remained completely silent.

Mariah ate only enough to help digest the medication she was taking, and Eli was too overwhelmed by fear and helplessness to even look at the food. He was out of ideas and knew they had to be smart to survive. Eli finally ate a few bites and then looked at Mariah and told her that they would continue the discussion in the car.

Eli started the engine but didn't back out. "Where do you think we should go?" he asked. It seemed to Eli that Mariah had suspended her breathing, and for a split second he panicked, thinking something was wrong.

Mariah placed her hand on Eli's leg, gave a confident but weak smile, and began explaining an idea she had been working on over breakfast. "I think we should get a few steps ahead of our adversary. We're about to travel to a place where we know they'll be looking for us, Alexandria, Egypt. So we must not look like ourselves.

"We have to have a secure place to come back to in Denver, one where we can leave the traveling gems. This evil knows all the places we've been, so we must be able to come back to somewhere that is safe and where we haven't been before.

Let's go downtown to check into a hotel where we can leave the car for a few days. Then we should visit the post office and secure a post-office box. Next we should buy some jewelry that comes in a small box. We will replace the jewelry with our traveling gems and mail them to our new post-office box. When we need to return to Denver, we will have a safe and secure landing zone protected by the government. I believe the post office building will be large enough for all of us to return to.

"Our next step will be to go shopping for clothes. We'll get a pleated and belted maxi dress for me and a whole new business look for you, so that when we travel we'll be less conspicuous. My dress should be long and roomy enough that I can hide the robe underneath."

Eli looked at her in amazement. She had thought of everything.

"When we've bought everything we need and mailed the box with the traveling gems in them, then we can robe to Alexandria together.

"What do you think?" With hardly a pause she continued. "Instead of the pillar, we will go to the new preplanned location where Avitus and his men helped Shamar find the Scroll of Knowledge."

Mariah leaned back in her seat. The conversation left her worn out and short of breath. She looked at Eli and gave a tired smile. Again she asked weakly, "What do you think?"

Eli thought for a while in astonishment and said that he liked her idea. *Why didn't I think of that? Although she is sick and weak, she came up with a better plan than I could have.* Pulling out onto the highway, Eli headed toward downtown to follow through with Mariah's plan.

They found a hotel close to the main post office and registered. "The first thing we need to do is get a PO box," Mariah said. They walked to the main post office and secured a post-office box. Although she still looked pale and was obviously weak, Eli observed that having a plan had injected new spirit into her actions.

"Now we need to get jewelry and clothing," Mariah stated, "with the clothing being first." Eli accompanied Mariah to a women's clothing store, where Mariah purchased the appropriate dress for their trip. Next they went to a men's shop and bought a suit for Eli. While there, Mariah also picked up two sets of cuff links that were packaged in a nice box.

Satisfied with their choices, Eli and Mariah went back to the post office, purchased wrapping paper and tape, went to a counter, and wrapped the gems in the cuff link box. They then proceeded to the mail clerk and mailed the gems to their new post-office box.

Their final step was all that remained, so they went to a coffee shop, where they rested and enjoyed a cup of tea and a pastry. Mariah excused herself, and taking her shopping bag, she went to the women's room to change clothes. When she arrived back at the table, Eli took his shopping bag and went to the men's room. He returned a little later, and together they both exited the coffee shop. While returning to their hotel, Eli and Mariah gave their old clothes to people begging on the street.

Arriving at their hotel, they hurried to their room as Eli continually looked up and down the hallway to notice if they were followed. He saw nothing.

After they entered their room, Mariah promptly grabbed a small backpack and then took the passports from her purse and put them inside Eli's jacket.

Mariah and Eli gave each other a kiss, and Eli softly said, "I'm ready to travel." Mariah said the prayer, and both were transported to modern-day Alexandria.

▲ ▲ ▲

Tony's phone rang, and he answered, interrupting his conversation with Donald. After listening and muttering a few words, he responded, "I'll be right down," and hung up. "FBI's here," he said to Donald. "Let's go escort him in."

The three of them engaged in small talk up to the office but went straight to work when they arrived, reviewing the security videos on both the flash drives. They fast-forwarded through much of the material, slowing down for the action scenes and sometimes replaying some of the segments in order to study the details.

When they finished, Donald displayed the map he had brought out of the bunker. "I sent the original map to Egypt but made several copies; you can have one, and I'm leaving copies here with the police and one for me and my office to share."

The agent stood and faced Tony and Donald. He had been mostly quiet during the review of the video clips and the map. After thinking for a few minutes, he chose his words carefully.

"The man in the costume is known by the FBI as Sago." He paused and watched Tony and Donald for a reaction. Seeing none, he cleared his throat and continued in a firm voice.

"This man is a big underworld crime boss who is known for dealing in stolen antiquities. It's odd to see him here doing his own dirty work and even stranger to see him in that costume. I presume he anticipated finding people there and didn't want to be recognized. I guess he's too proud to wear a sweatshirt and hoodie like a common criminal.

"Have you spoken to the doctor?" he asked.

"We haven't found him yet. We're still trying to identify him," Tony answered.

"This looks like it's in our jurisdiction since it involves kidnapping, so we'll take charge. I need to talk to the young lady's parents and to the butler. It's important that we know why she was kidnapped and whether any ransom was requested. You had mentioned that her father worked at a local museum. I wonder whether that fact, along with the map you found, indicates they were after something other than money."

"We thought that as well," Tony said. "That's why we invited Don here, from INTERPOL.

"Unfortunately, since the body was found, we haven't been able to contact any of them. We detained some of them here before the crime was discovered. They had been falsely blamed for a convenience store robbery that turned out to be an amateurish attempt at framing them. It seems now that there must be some relationship between that incident and the kidnapping. A complete report of everything we told you is included in the files we're giving you.

"We don't know where any of them are," he repeated. "They disappeared. None of them are home or at work, and nobody who knows them seems to know anything. Notes on those efforts are also included in your files."

Showing a slight inability to focus, the agent slowly responded, "Odd." He shook their hands, thanked them, and gathered up the map and the flash drives. "I'll be in touch," he said, and then he left.

Several minutes after the FBI agent left Tony's office, Tony's voice betrayed a mild feeling of excitement as he turned to Donald and said, "Big-time crime boss! Possible interest in international antiquities and a kidnapping! Do you think INTERPOL might have this Sago person's name in their database?"

With a light-hearted teasing in his voice, Donald smiled back at Tony and said, "My thought too. I would be so pleased to inquire for you. I'm very intrigued with this case and would like it if you will allow me to see it to its completion." Tony smiled back at him and extended his hand, giving Donald a firm handshake.

The new team member beamed as he delivered his report to Vincent, describing a perfect con. He continued by explaining how he picked up on the text Shamar sent from his cell phone to Eli, and by homing in on the GPS he could determine where Shamar and Sophia were.

Continuing, he added confidently that Addison, Gabriel, Sophia, and Shamar were all together and would be bringing him all their artifacts.

He gave a brief description of their encounter and passionately he stated how he convinced them that he was the shomer and that he did it so effectively that they all not only believed, but were elated to gather the artifacts and help him and were even concerned about his safety. They had made an arrangement to meet him tomorrow night at the pillar.

Upon completing his verbal report, he smiled at Vincent.

Vincent was thoroughly pleased with the information and began preparing for the encounter. He told his men to be staked out in the area near the pillar tomorrow night before nine.

Vincent was about to contact the phantom when one of the phantom's surrogates materialized. He told Vincent that the phantom was pleased with this new development and that he would be there tomorrow night to claim the artifacts himself and take care of the guests. This surrogate waited for no response but disappeared as quickly as he had appeared.

Twelve

TRUST

Gabriel and Addison rejoined Sophia and Shamar. Addison summarized their work: "We sent a telegram to Eli and Mariah at their motel, warning them about their cell phones. And Gabriel placed all our cell phones in the lobby of two different hotels. He positioned them in potted plants so that noise from the lobby could be picked up but would be so muffled that listeners couldn't make out what was being said."

Sophia and Shamar remained seated on the stone bench a slight distance from Gabriel and Addison.

Feeling the distrust in the air, Addison cautiously began explaining his relationship with Sago. "Sophia, I want to answer your question concerning Sago and me. Sago was adopted by my parents after his mother and father died, and so we were raised together.

"We never had a close relationship because we had such different attitudes about almost everything; however, we respected each other, and for some reason Sago made sure that his criminal activity never overflowed into my life. "That is," he corrected himself, "until now.

"Sago went his way after high school, and I went mine. Yes, I knew in the bunker that it was Sago who was in costume, but I was afraid that you would have the same reaction that you just displayed when you learned of our relationship, so I kept quiet.

"Regardless of what took place at the bunker and the compound where you were held captive, Sophia, Sago has twice taken great risk for you; actually, for all of us.

"The first was by having his men allow you to escape the compound, and the second was here, by warning us about our cell phones and the extreme danger our lives are in.

"I'm certain that he's paying the ultimate price, and I believe he chose to atone for what he has done wrong in his life by making sure we were safe. I also believe that somewhere within Sago he still holds affection for his stepbrother, and he was not going to let anyone harm me or my friends."

He choked on these last words and broke his eye contact with them as he looked at the ground to hide his tears.

Clearing his throat he continued. "I feel that I am dredging up history and trying to understand how it led here. Sago chose, Sophia, *chose* to do the right thing. I am proud of him for that choice, and I regret that I can never let him know just how much I appreciate what he gave up for us. I do hope he saw the gratitude and sorrow in my eyes as he was leaving."

Gabriel, Shamar, and Sophia were speechless. There was a long, awkward silence. Finally Shamar said, "I'm sorry for your loss, Addison. I believe we can repay Sago's support and sacrifice by being victorious in this quest. For now, I think that means that we must find a way to get to Taposiris."

Extending his arm to Sophia, Shamar said, "Come, we must go. There is much to be done, and I will not leave your side." Everyone solemnly turned around and quietly began walking back toward the Citadel's harbor. Shamar and Sophia walked together, and Gabriel and Addison walked together.

Addison still had the unshakeable sense that Sophia and Shamar didn't trust him, and he was wondering whether Gabriel felt the same. *How can I be helpful if they believe they can't trust me?*

While walking, Addison turned his attention to the surrounding area, noticing that numerous boats offered private tours and fishing expeditions.

As everyone quietly ate their breakfast, Addison kept a watchful eye on the people who worked around this area, especially a nearby man who was standing close to a boat with a sign stating that he offered individual or personal tours.

Addison turned to everyone and exclaimed, "Let's take a boat to Taposiris! I don't think they will be looking for us to travel by boat, and I believe it will be a quicker way to reach our destination. I still have a feeling that the rabbi knew of or had something there that we must find."

Sophia and Shamar discussed the proposal and said that they agreed, and Addison led the way to the boat. Gabriel had been looking elsewhere while listening to Sophia and Shamar make their decision. He could feel the tension rising between Sophia and Addison, and he didn't like it and didn't want to make anyone uncomfortable, so he remained silent and just followed along.

Shamar and Sophia followed Addison down to the man who offered his boat for rent. Gabriel, searching internally for answers rather than asking questions, placed himself between Addison and the couple. This hostility boded poorly for their future. Personally he didn't believe Addison had betrayed them and felt bad for everyone's ill feelings. So he chose to remain close to Addison and protect him.

As Addison approached to the man with the small boat, he waved, getting the man's attention, and then they engaged in negotiating the payment for transportation for four passengers to the Golden Beach North Coast.

The man told Addison that it would take an hour and a half or perhaps two hours. The fare was paid, and all boarded the small boat. Gabriel commented on how cozy the seating arrangement was. But no one responded.

The boat had rocked gently as they were seated and then began undulating as they pulled out. Crossing the wakes of other boats in the harbor was too much for Sophia; she was already tired and weak from a sleepless night and strange foods. The boat's captain, noticing her pale face and apparent nausea, reduced the speed and offered her a bottle of water, some pills, and a few tissues.

After two hours of traveling in silence, they were all relieved as they viewed their destination and approached the shore.

Arriving at the beach, their guide had no problem navigating his boat up to the beach.

The four disembarked, and Addison gave the guide a tip and thanked him for his assistance.

Their boat guide pointed up at the hill and then shouted back confirmation that before them was Taposiris. He added that it was approximately a thousand meters from the beach to the entrance of the ruins of the ancient Temple.

Everyone paused as they looked ahead toward the top of a small hill. Addison could see a portion of the ruins almost straight ahead of them. However, as his eyes moved across the landscape to where the ancient ruins of the main gate, he surmised that this walk would be rough, as there were no sidewalks, handrails, pathways, or roads.

Addison and Gabriel led the way up the long pathway toward the ruins. They picked their way leisurely, enjoying a light breeze. The route they took started off sandy and gradually transformed into sand mixed with fragments of sharp rocks and stone.

Everyone's progress slowed down dramatically as the terrain became harsher, and their feet were hot from the sand.

The stroll took almost thirty minutes to bring them to the once grand opening into the compound of Taposiris. Sophia and Shamar were amazed at the changes that had occurred over the past fourteen hundred years. They struggled to identify features that they could recognize from their previous visit.

Everyone paused for a moment, catching their breath and surveying the surrounding area. "What a hike!" Shamar added, looking back at the direction they had just walked. "I'm glad we're finally here."

Slowly they all strolled in together through the ruins before them.

"Hey, you! Stop!" A voice broke the silence as they entered the ruin, startling everyone.

They all quickly turned toward the source of the shouting. Gabriel recognized the man who was yelling at them; it was the same man he had met on his wild misadventure in his panic-stricken excursion back and forth through time.

The man continued speaking to Gabriel as he swiftly approached him. With annoyance in his voice he said, "It's you again! And don't disappear this time!"

Lowering his voice and leaning toward Gabriel, the young man quizzically looked at the others and then continued. "We have very little time left to get there and perform the ceremony because you are so late. Where is the rabbi?"

Before anyone could say anything, the ground began to shake; however, this time it was not a small shake but one in which the ground moved with such force that they grabbed at each other for balance, as they all had difficulty standing upright while swaying with the movement of the earth.

Addison remarked, "I think that was a four or five on the Richter scale."

The young man commented during the earth's movement, "This is a sign from Lucifer himself that he is preparing to make his grand entrance. We must hurry and perform the ceremony."

There was complete silence, and then Gabriel spoke up and told Addison, Shamar, and Sophia that this was the man he saw when he was having trouble remembering which prayer to use.

Seeing the surprised look on everyone's face, the young man took a step back from the group. With an inquisitive voice, he asked again, "Where is the rabbi? I hope he arrives soon."

No one in the group made an attempt to answer his question. Gabriel took a step forward and introduced them all to him. Then he asked, "Who am I speaking to, and what's the name of the rabbi you are expecting?"

There was a long pause as the young man stood up straight. With a cautious voice, he said, "Moses, my name is Moses." He did not answer the other question.

Gabriel asked again, "Moses, please tell us the name of the rabbi you are seeking."

Speaking slowly and cautiously, as if needing time to choose his words, Moses stated, "I am Moses Cohen; my home is in Israel. I am an archeological student. I was to meet my mother's cousin, Rabbi Benjamin Katz here at Taposiris."

A surge of hope rushed through Addison, followed quickly by a brief bout of despair as he wondered whether this might be another fake shomer. With his hopes diminished, Addison worried that this chance encounter might be yet another mishap.

Apparently, others felt just as Addison did because Sophia, in a less than polite voice, spoke up. "Moses, Rabbi Katz is dead." Everyone watched, waiting to see how Moses responded to the news.

Moses's face turned pale, and he appeared to be on the verge of collapse. With a quiet, strained voice, he meekly said, "No. No, that can't be. I pray that you are wrong. Without the rabbi we are doomed; humankind is condemned."

A few minutes of silence passed, and Moses solemnly asked, "When did he die?" and quickly added, "He is, was, or rather, together we were to perform the ceremony. I volunteered to be his assistant. I come from a long line of shomers; my family was bound to keep and protect certain secrets and items that Benjamin needed. I assisted him to the best of my abilities while he explored archeological sites for some of the missing items.

"Benjamin also studied in preparation for this ceremony. Unless one of you is qualified or has the necessary knowledge to fill in for him, we are in serious trouble, and this may now be an ill-fated venture, after which humanity will be cursed."

Taking a deep breath before he continued, Moses asked, "What about his artifacts? Did someone recover them?"

Addison, still unsure of their situation, guardedly said, "He passed recently on his way home from the synagogue. The coroner said it was a heart attack. As for artifacts…" He paused due to the sensitivity of their position, and hesitantly continued. "He sent several to some of us. I don't know if we have them all."

Shamar started to say something when Moses raised his hand signaling for not just Shamar but everyone not to speak.

Moses looked around and softly said, "Don't say any more out here in public. It seems deserted here, but it might not be. There are others here who must not know who you are, and especially that you have arrived to meet me.

We can't take any risk that our conversation might be overheard and must guard that no one gains knowledge of anything we have to discuss.

"There is a double-wide trailer just around the corner. I've been staying in it with several other archeological students from Israel while we were here studying this site.

"My friends all went back to Israel. I stayed behind, waiting for Benjamin. My life is in great danger without the company of my fellow Jews. I knew of the danger when I chose to stay, but I never anticipated the rabbi not showing up.

"Come, follow me. Let's go to where we can speak in private. We're not safe out here."

Moses's brows drew closer, and his face tightened. Looking toward Addison he drew in a deep breath, and as he released it, added, "And I don't believe Benjamin had a heart attack; more likely he was murdered to make sure we couldn't proceed with the ceremony."

Moses started to lead the way but quickly spun around and faced the group. He leaned side to side and continued looking all around. With a slight shakiness in his voice, he whispered, "Were you followed?"

Moses looked at each of them for a response to his question. Seeing blank faces he quickly blurted out in despair, "Our lives are in deeper danger than I had anticipated, and crafty, evil people will continue to disrupt our efforts and you"—his hand swept through the air as he motioned toward the group— "none of you know if you were followed!"

Turning quickly, Moses resumed walking toward his trailer. Glancing back at the group, he watched to see what they would do.

Shamar and Sophia were hesitant, but Addison and Gabriel were already moving right behind him.

Shamar and Sophia reluctantly followed them to the trailer. Everything that had taken place since their arrival at Taposiris was not at all what they expected to experience when they found the shomer.

Moses took the keys from his pocket as he approached the trailer steps, and he unlocked the door and motioned for everyone to enter. After everyone had gone into the trailer, he entered too and locked the door behind him.

Moses stopped briefly and then gestured for everyone to have a seat. He offered food and water and tea. He also asked that they speak in low voices and for no one to speak loud, as it would bring attention to the trailer, which was supposed to have only one occupant.

Everyone sat down on the couch and chairs and anxiously waited as Moses began explaining his relationship with Rabbi Katz. "The rabbi is my mother's cousin. He approached my mother almost a year and a half ago and said that a certain item had been discovered, along with other signs that his family had been instructed to watch for.

"That is when Benjamin began gathering all that was necessary to perform a ceremony to defeat a demon who wishes to gain control over humanity. Benjamin said this demon would use deceit and cunning to prevent him and everyone else associated with the ceremony from being successful.

"Let me get for you the letters I have from him about this project."

There was a short period of silence. Moses stopped, turned to face everyone, and stated, "This isn't how it's supposed to be. I understood Benjamin to state that a rabbi must be present at the ceremony, and now we don't have one. Additionally we need all the artifacts he was collecting, and you don't know if you have them. Great!

"I'm frightened since none of you seem to know anything about what is necessary to perform the ceremony and you have admitted that none of you can perform the ceremony. Yet, here you are. And here I am. And we must, one way or another, save the world. Scary, isn't it?"

Moses walked to a small, locked chest, unlocked it, and grabbed a handful of letters, taking them to the group. Sophia immediately grabbed the stack as he set the letters down on a coffee table.

Moses repeated his belief that he didn't think they could be successful with the ceremony without the necessary guidance from the rabbi. "And," he added, "we need special robes, four of them, along with matching flasks."

Moses took one particular letter from Sophia and pointed to the instructions from Benjamin about the robes and flasks. "Apparently the rabbi sent more detailed instructions to Mr. Eli Daniels. I need to contact Mr. Daniels and see if he has the information we need."

Sophia looked at the letters, comparing in her mind what she remembered of the rabbi's writing. These definitely seemed to be letters that could have been written by the rabbi.

Moses, adjusting to the realization that their chance of success seemed hopeless, stated in a low voice, "I was to meet Benjamin here at Taposiris and then together we would travel to Jordan to perform the ceremony."

"Jordan!" repeated everyone in unison. "Why there?"

Nodding his head as if he wasn't surprised at all, Moses became quiet and a solemn look of wonder flashed across his face. Shamar looked at Moses's facial expression and asked if something was wrong.

Moses began slowly backing away from the group and softly, in a cautious voice, replied to Shamar. "I don't know who you are and have taken you at your word, and now it seems as if none of you know anything. How can you be who you say you are if you don't know the most basic of the necessary details?"

Moses became despondent. He sensed that he had shared way too much information with these strangers, and now he had serious doubts about that choice.

Addison immediately spoke up. "Yes, we are somewhat uninformed as to what needs to be done, as well as the where and why of this operation. However, the rabbi sent clues for us to follow, not realizing that we lacked enough knowledge to understand completely what needed to be done.

"Nevertheless, we continued to try and understand what to do, and we've made a lot of progress—that includes finding you. He left us almost no information about where you would be. It's possible he left out the details for fear that we might accidentally divulge them."

Addison hesitated for a moment as he tried to interpret the expressions on Moses's face, and then he continued solemnly. "We are doing this based on the relationship that Eli Daniels had with Rabbi Katz. Sophia here is the daughter of Eli and Mariah Daniels, and the rest of us are friends of the Daniels. All of us have the deepest respect for the rabbi and his desire that this pursuit be followed through to its very end.

"The only thing that we are certain of is that an evil beyond anything we were prepared for is right on our heels; furthermore, this evil is prepared to kill us for what we have and what they think we know."

Moses interrupted Addison. "I'm sorry. I'm having trouble making sense of all this; none of you knows how to perform the ceremony, and none of you knew where this ceremony is to be held, and yet, and yet you are telling me that Benjamin asked you to step in for him to complete this mission, without giving you any details?"

Moses stopped speaking and began pacing in the living room. Looking directly at Addison, Moses spoke up again. "Something tells me that if you were from the devil, you would have killed me and taken what you wanted. However, you must have items that evil desires, if I understand you correctly, and evildoers are trying to stop you from being successful. Tell me, how do I know that the items you have brought are the actual artifacts needed for the ceremony?"

There was a solemn silence for several moments as everyone digested all that had just been stated. Then the silence was interrupted by Gabriel who said, "These robes, flasks, and scrolls have been acquired at a great cost, Moses, and one was the death of Rabbi Katz. When Rabbi Katz passed this challenge to Mr. Daniels, Eli didn't know what this quest entailed, but he accepted it because he wanted to support his friend the rabbi."

Something finally clicked, and Moses looked excited, understanding that these people were connected with Eli Daniels. He remembered that Benjamin had spoken of Mr. Daniels several times, saying that he had immense trust and faith in Eli and his family.

Gabriel hesitantly continued, repeating to Moses that Sophia was the daughter of Eli and Mariah Daniels and adding that he, Sophia, Shamar, and Addison had all arrived in Alexandria, Egypt, to follow through on the rabbi's request to find the shomer at Taposiris. And that their arrival to modern-day Alexandria was accomplished through the use of the robes.

Moses apologized again and stated, "Let me explain to you the knowledge given to me by Benjamin of the situation: Lucifer wants to show God that he can and will restore and rebuild Sodom and Gomorrah—in Jordan, near the Dead Sea—making it his command headquarters and that from that site he will control humanity from a place once destroyed by God for its wickedness.

"This demon chose Sodom and Gomorrah because these were two of the most disgusting cities in the known world, in which God was so offended with the people's wicked ways that he destroyed them with fire and brimstone.

"So this demon wants to prove to God that humanity is still greedy, immoral, and power hungry, and the devil wants to prove that he can persuade humanity to become as evil as or worse than those who occupied Sodom and Gomorrah at the time of their destruction."

As trust was beginning to build, the visitors began asking questions, and Moses answered them all to the best of his ability.

Shamar thought it appropriate to bring Moses up to date on how each of them was brought into this project, what had transpired, and what they knew about the quest. He started at the beginning, and the others assisted, expressing their experiences and thoughts during the conversation.

Moses asked if they had the flasks and robes. Addison said that they had three of the four flasks but that they had not found the original phoenix flask and adding that he and Gabriel had obtained a substitute. He further stated that the rabbi had a duplicate of each robe made according to directions from a rabbi in ancient Alexandria and with gems provided by that rabbi. Addison added his opinion that he believed that these robes were to be used in the ceremony.

Moses asked if he could see the robes. Shamar revealed the dragon robe; Gabriel showed him the snake robe that he was wearing and reached into the seamstress's bag, which he had secured at his side, and fumbled around trying to grasp the Phoenix robe. With a sudden stiffening of his posture, Gabriel tried to speak. The pitch and volume of his voice was weak as he muttered, "The bag is empty."

Distraught again, Moses demanded, "How could you lose it? Do you know how, where, or when you lost the phoenix robe?" And where is the robe of scrolls?"

Addison was shocked that the phoenix robe was missing, but he quickly interjected that the scroll robe was with Eli and Mariah and that their last communication with them was to meet the group where Shamar found the Scroll of Knowledge. "They might be there now," he added.

He continued explaining that Eli and Mariah were to meet Addison or Sophia or Gabriel when they arrived at the prearranged place. However, since that arrangement, it was discovered that evil sources had compromised their cell phones, and now they no longer had means to communicate with each other.

Addison said, "I used Western Union to inform the Daniels about the cell phones and the new meeting place."

Distressed, Gabriel was in a state of absolute panic, and he began tossing everything on the floor, examining and reexamining the debris to find the phoenix robe. It wasn't anywhere. His body tensed up while he recalled the last place he remembered seeing it; it was at the shaved-ice stand. He thought to himself, *I hope the fake shomer didn't take it.*

There was a solemn moment, and finally Moses spoke. "Shamar, let's go to the place where you are to meet Eli and Mariah before someone or something else can intervene. Everyone else, wait here until we get back. It's about a ninety-minute round trip, and if Eli and Mariah have already arrived, we can be in and out of that area quickly."

Moses ceased moving and turned toward everyone. Feeling a sense of kinship with the others, he smiled and said, "The loss of your phones is not the catastrophe you think. There is something that Rabbi Katz shared with me while he visited our home. Once, I had wondered how the rabbi knew where I was and what I was doing, so I asked him how he knew. He smiled and said that while he was in ancient Alexandria, the rabbi there explained to him the attributes of the yellow gems.

"If you desire to hear or view a person, well you can do that with the use of yellow gems.

"Just hold the gem in the palm of your hand or put the palm of your hand over the gem, and request which robe or person you wish to communicate with. You can see and hear what is happening around the person wearing that particular robe.

"Other gems have similar properties. Blue ones, ususally sapphires or jacinth, can communicate with anyone wearing a robe with those gems. And the bright red sardius gems are good at sending and receiving messages."

This new information surprised them all.

As Moses was handing the key to the trailer to Addison, he instructed him to lock the door behind them.

"We sure could have used that information earlier," Gabriel said. Then his face brightened as he realized the implications for the present. He exclaimed, "Let's try it now! Get the yellow gems, and we'll look for the robe of scrolls. That'll tell us where Eli and Mariah are."

Addison grabbed a handful of yellow gems that were on Gabriel's snake robe and held them firmly in the palm of his hand. Gabriel and Sophia both concentrated on the robe of scrolls, and Gabriel concentrated on the phoenix robe. After staring for a few moments, Sophia said excitedly, "I see my mother."

She watched a little longer, and her face paled. "Mother looks different. She's wearing unusual clothing, and she looks sick."

Sophia continued studying the surrounding details and cheered up again saying, "They're near the Temple of Canopus. You need to go now," she said. And Shamar and Moses quickly departed.

As the others watched them leave, Gabriel was using the yellow gem and blurted out that he saw the phoenix robe but couldn't quite make out who was wearing it. Whoever had it was in a slightly secluded area with trees, and there were bushes around them.

Thirteen

FAILURE AND REUNION

Anxious about the night's meeting, Vincent had anticipation of full re-demption. Capturing all the people of interest except for the shomer and securing all the artifacts should really please the phantom. Once they had everything, the shomer would be irrelevant.

Delirious with excitement, he twirled quickly in his chair and leaned over and grasped the phone. He pushed the button to contact his security de-tail and asked them to provide for him all the information gleaned from the bugged phones overnight.

"There has been activity all night on all the phones, the security guard answered. "We couldn't understand most of it, since it was muffled by some-thing. However, all the phones are still in two hotels, and my men have placed surveillance on each of them."

Vincent told his men to go into each hotel and, keeping a low profile, watch the targets and try to learn whether they had gathered all the items for the ceremony.

Less than ten minutes had passed when the security team reported back to Vincent that they had entered the hotels and discovered that the targets had never checked in and were nowhere to be seen. However, they did find the cell phones. The phones had been left in various spots about the lobby of each hotel, and that is why they heard voices all night.

Vincent was furious. *How did they find out about the phones? Somebody will pay dearly for this breach.* He told the supervisors to have an immediate roll call and find out who might be missing, also to check to make sure they all had their cell phones. He wanted the leak found and plugged. Next he ordered the men to begin checking all restaurants and public places for the four of them.

Vincent then contacted Robert and asked him to recount exactly what had taken place during his meeting with Addison, Shamar, Gabriel, and Sophia.

After listening to Robert, Vincent realized that his life was over. He had reassured the phantom that everything was under control, and now it wasn't. Jumping to his feet and sprinting toward the front door, all Vincent could think of was the importance of taking control as quickly as possible. Opening the door he saw before him the phantom, Senka, and two of the phantom's servants. Senka was wearing a tight-fitting dog collar around her neck with the end of the leash tightly clutched in the phantom's hand.

With a swift movement of the phantom's free hand, Vincent was no longer there. An imperceptible gasp escaped Senka's lips, but she was careful not to let the phantom discover her true feelings. She had liked Vincent but dared not let the phantom know.

"Tell everyone I'm taking charge," the phantom directed to his two companions, "and tell them to watch all major ancient ruins and hotels, restaurants, airports, and bus stations, as well as land routes in and out of Egypt. And, most important, remind them of the price of failure."

▲ ▲ ▲

Moses and Shamar traveled down the highway in Moses's van. Almost an hour had passed, and Moses was finally able to pull into a parking space close to the entrance of the Temple of Canopus. "Lock your door," he reminded Shamar, "and let's stay close together."

Knowing there could be spies in the area, Moses moved briskly to Shamar's side and said, "You know Mariah and Eli and I don't, so when you see them, approach them cautiously and as discreetly as possible. We can't draw attention to ourselves."

Shamar shook his head in agreement and added, "If you see someone suspicious, let me know, and we'll figure something out together."

Moses and Shamar walked around looking for Eli and Mariah but didn't see them anywhere in the public area in front of the cave. "Let's go in," Shamar suggested, "since they might have tried to hide there. It was within this cave that I had found the scroll, so they could be waiting in that part of the cave."

They both entered the cave and concentrated on the path Shamar had used with Avitus and his men. Moses gagged a few times due to the foul stench as Shamar led the way. They walked to the place where the scroll had been found and, finding no one there, returned to the entrance.

Eli and Mariah had been walking around the small pond for almost an hour looking for Addison, Gabriel, Sophia, or Shamar. At last Mariah spotted Shamar departing the cave and hustled toward him. She could tell that he didn't recognize her, so she called out to him, saying, "Hello, sweetheart, your father and I are over here."

Shamar was surprised, and at first he was startled at the sight of an older Egyptian woman rushing at him, but then he recognized her voice. Her disguise was perfect. Mariah put her arms around Shamar and said, "My son, how are you doing?"

Shamar gave Mariah a big hug and responded, "Fine, Mom. How are you and Dad doing? Mom, I'd like you to meet my friend, Al. Where's Dad?" Then he bent down and quietly whispered, "The man with me is Moses, the shomer."

Mariah responded that they were fine and so glad that they could catch up with them. She looked at Moses and said, "I'm glad to meet you. Shamar has told us so much about you, and I am glad that you're here to greet us too."

Eli joined them, and Mariah exclaimed, "Eli, this is Al, who came with our son to meet us." Before Eli could shake hands, Mariah pulled his head over and whispered, "This is Moses, the shomer."

After a quick double-take, Eli caught on and said, "Glad to meet you. Thank you for coming with our son."

After a short pause, Shamar put his arm around Mariah, and the four of them walked back to Moses's van and began the return trip to Taposiris.

"What a great disguise, Mariah," Shamar remarked. "I didn't recognize you at all."

Mariah asked how everyone was, and Shamar answered, stating that they were all fine but that they needed to gather as a group and focus on all the recent developments. "A lot has changed, and since we finally found the real shomer, we have learned a lot."

Then, seeing confusion on all their faces, Shamar realized that none of them knew about the fake shomer. He explained that episode briefly and then summarized what they had learned about Addison and Sago's relationship, and then advised them of the missing phoenix robe. "We can go into more detail once we get back to the trailer."

Eli had been listening in and added a comment. "Good. Even I have new information, as I finally read the rabbi's last communication."

There was a long pause, and then Moses casually remarked that Mariah's covering of the robe was great and that he considered it a brilliant way to arrive inconspicuously and keep their identities and the robe hidden. "What the rabbi told me about you, Eli, was encouraging. I look forward to joining forces with all of you."

Moses peeked into the rearview mirror and noticed that Eli was watching their surroundings, taking notice of everyone and everything around them. He was glad to see that Eli and Mariah were so much more cautious than the others.

Fourteen

THE FINAL JOURNEY BEGINS

When they arrived at the trailer, Moses asked everyone to wait in the van. He approached the trailer and gently knocked. There was no response. Listening at the door, Moses heard nothing. While knocking again he placed his face very close to the door and softly spoke. "It's me—Moses. Please open the door." No response again, and as before, there was silence.

Moses looked around at the ground and then back at the van, and realized that Eli, Shamar, and Mariah were all watching him.

A cold chill shot down Moses's spine as he wondered what could have gone wrong. His heart raced, and his forehead became wet with sweat, as he feared the worst had happened and that evil had followed them here after all because of their lack of caution.

He looked around again, and again saw nothing. "This is it!" he said to himself. "They have caught up with us." He surveyed the surrounding area for signs of the imminent ambush that he knew must be coming.

His emotions shifted to panic, and he wanted to flee, but he knew he couldn't. No matter how careless their actions were, they were his only hope to help save the future of humankind.

He turned to face the van and wiped his hand across his forehead to get rid of the sweat. His legs were wobbly as he shuffled back to the van. Opening the door Moses blurted out, "I told them to stay here." He paused to glance around for signs of danger again, and then continued with excitement in his voice, screeching, "And yet they all seem to be gone. I don't know why they'd leave, unless the evil ones caught up with them. They didn't seem to be very observant of their surroundings before, and they didn't even try to make sure that they weren't being followed."

Eli quickly and firmly stated, "Moses, get into the van so we can talk about this."

Entering the van, Moses's hand shook uncontrollably as he grabbed the steering wheel. His voice was lower and quavered with fright as he explained what had just taken place. "I have a bad feeling about this," he said. "I'm really worried and scared too!"

Obviously annoyed at Gabriel's, Sophia's, and Addison's apparent impulsiveness and lack of caution, an agitated Eli demanded more details. "Did it look like the trailer had been forcibly entered, or were there signs of a struggle?" he asked, edging forward on his seat as he spoke.

Mariah remained speechless, but Eli and Shamar both knew her silence meant that she was deep in thought.

Wanting to calm the situation, Shamar started to speak but was preempted by Mariah, who spoke up in a strong motherly voice. "We must think rationally and not make snap judgments. I'm positive there is an explanation for them not being here."

Eli repeated his question to Moses about evidence of a struggle.

"No," Moses quickly responded. After a brief pause, Moses added, "It didn't look like anyone broke into the trailer, and I didn't see any extra footprints in the sand around the door, so I guess they went somewhere on their own."

Shamar reminded everyone about the new information from Moses with reference to the yellow gems. "We're not without clues," he said. Let's try Moses's new information about the yellow gems on our robes and try and see Gabriel, Addison, and Sophia. We should be able to see where they are and hear what's going on around them. So, we haven't lost total contact with them."

Mariah asked Shamar to come close to her so they could use some of the yellow gems on his robe; she sensed his robe was stronger than hers.

Shamar and Mariah each grasped some yellow gems, and they concentrated on the missing people.

After concentrating for a few minutes, Mariah was relieved to see all three of the missing travelers in an area that resembled a small park. She promptly relayed to everyone that she saw Sophia, and that she and the others appeared to be OK. "They are near some stone benches."

Shamar hastily said, "Let's all group together so we can robe there immediately."

"No!" Mariah snapped.

Shocked by her outburst, everyone became silent.

Moses placed both hands on the steering wheel and quietly said, "Oh no." He was certain that Mariah was about to scold all of them because she sounded just like a distressed mother.

Mariah first looked at Moses and then turned to Eli and Shamar to explain her outburst. "Sophia, Gabriel, and Addison seem to be OK for now; thank God they don't appear to be captives. Nevertheless, if we all just pop in and it's a trap, evil will have all of us. Maybe evil convinced them to go to this area to meet us. We should try to use telepathy to communicate to them to seek shelter as quickly as possible and that they must make sure there's no one following them. We also should instruct them to wait for further instructions from us.

"Perhaps they can get to the Temple of Canopus and hide in the tunnels," she added. "It is essential for all of us to think before we act, or we could screw everything up."

Shamar looked down at his folded hands and added his analysis. "Indeed it seems we have at least three possible actions we could take, and none of them are good. We can choose to wait here and hope they can get back to the trailer undetected. Or perhaps we can drive to where we think they are and hope we find them while at the same time we attempt to stay undetected. Or we may select to robe to where they are, and hope there is no ambush waiting for us."

Now clasping his hands together so tightly that his knuckles were white, Shamar continued. "I think I know where they are, and I understand why they are there. The place I saw while using the gems looked like the area around the shaved-ice shop where we met the fake shomer and Sago. My guess is that they robed back there to look for the phoenix robe. Gabriel felt really bad when he realized he lost it."

Everyone heard Moses firmly and matter-of-factly state, "What a foolish thing to do."

Each was silent, and then Mariah cautiously asked, "How far from the Temple of Canopus is the place where you believe they are, Shamar?"

"Around a mile give or take a little," he responded. And then he asked, "Why?"

Mariah turned to face Eli and Shamar, who were in the back seat. "I think they need to seek shelter at the temple and that they need to meet us there as quickly as possible. Can we try and communicate this to them?"

Shamar leaned forward so that Mariah could grasp the gems on his robe as he answered, "Yes." Together they began attempting to communicate with the others.

Mariah kept Sophia in her mind and was expressing to her daughter, "Go to the Temple of Canopus as quickly as possible and seek shelter where Shamar found the Scroll of Knowledge."

Shamar tried in the same way to contact Gabriel, and he was disclosing to him, "Seek shelter at Temple of Canopus tunnels, and be quick about it."

A few minutes had passed, and nothing happened. Shamar and Mariah felt like they failed. Moses started the engine and said, "We need to get away from here and find a place of protection."

Moses began backing up and turned the van to face the road to Alexandria.

Shamar spoke up. "Moses, can you park close to Pompey's Pillar of or find a place close enough that we can leave your van and walk?

Eli shocked everyone with a loud and resounding, "No, no, no, no, and no. Because evil will be looking for us there, and it would in effect be surrendering to them. We need to seek another solution. I like Mariah's idea to meet up at the Temple of Canopus. We have no time for side trips and must make up for lost time." Turning his attention to Moses, he said, "Moses, get us to the Temple of Canopus."

Moses continued traveling toward Alexandria. Shamar looked to Mariah for a split second and each immediately said, "Addison." Together they grasped yellow gems on Shamar's robe and began attempting to transmit their plans to Addison.

Moses spoke up. "I know a safe place where we can park the van and then walk the rest of the way to the Temple of Canopus."

Eli said, "Good. Do that now."

▲ ▲ ▲

Sophia didn't feel good about their choice to teleport to the phoenix robe. When they landed on the ground, she immediately said to Gabriel, "I still think this is a bad idea, and I want you to know that the only reason I'm here is because I didn't want to be left alone in that trailer.

"I think we have learned something already—since we haven't been approached, it seems that the robe wasn't stolen as bait for an ambush," she said sarcastically. Quickly she added, "That is, unless they're hiding out of sight, waiting for everyone else to show up."

Gabriel was half listening to Sophia while he studied their surroundings. Looking to Addison, Gabriel slowly and quietly said, "I believe the robe should be right here; I know for certain we're close because I can feel its essence pulsating through my robe.

"Sophia, look for a spot where you can keep a lookout while we search, and you can warn us of anything suspicious.

"Addison, I need you to search the ground around the benches and also take a peek into the trash bins to see if it was dropped or disposed of.

"I'm going to explore the area around these hedges."

Sophia dutifully went to a bench that overlooked the majority of the area and sat down to keep watch as instructed. Addison strolled by each bench, seeking clues that the robe might have been there or in the area. He also glanced into the trash bins as he passed them.

After a few moments, Sophia saw Gabriel drop to the ground and grab his ankle. She rushed to him to find out what was wrong. Arriving at his side, she was surprised to see he was only feigning an injury. As she pretended to examine his ankle, Gabriel was saying, "Keep Addison away from here. I see the robe just under the thick bushes to my left. And I believe it's wrapped around a body. I think its Sago. Apparently he put on the robe before he died. I need to somehow get to his body and retrieve the robe."

Sophia looked into the bush and could see Sago's body. Her chin quivered, and she tearfully whimpered. Gabriel quickly grabbed her and said, "I should have told you not to look; I'm sorry." She looked into Gabriel's eyes but said nothing. He just wanted to hold her and tell her it would be all right, but he knew she regretted her final remarks to Sago and now realized his sacrifice and that she couldn't apologize for her last words to him.

Tenderly he said, "You must go and find Addison and keep him busy for me so that I can retrieve the robe."

Slowly Sophia arose and glanced around, wondering where Addison was.

Gabriel said, "Crawling into the shrubs and then pulling the robe off of him will take some time. Can you distract Addison for a while? I don't want him to see this."

Sophia responded, "I'll tell Addison that I need to check out the area where the shomer came from, and that I don't want to go alone. I might be able to buy you ten or fifteen minutes to do what you need to do."

With that said Sophia hurried away and finally spotted Addison in the distance. She caught up with him, saying, "I'd like to retrace the fake shomers steps, from when Gabriel first saw him, to see if he left any clues. Could you please come with me? I don't want to be alone."

Addison was surprised at Sophia's change of heart, and with happiness in his voice, he initiated physical contact with Sophia, offering his arm so he could escort her. The two of them went arm in arm up a small hill to view the area where they thought the fake shomer had come from.

While they were occupied with the phony search, Gabriel got down on his knees and clawed his way into the bushes, pretending to look for something lost in the hedge. He viewed the body and confirmed it was Sago. Stopping for a moment, Gabriel said a prayer and thanked Sago for his sacrifice.

Moving closer to the body, Gabriel realized that removing the robe wasn't going to be easy, and it would be even harder to leave behind the remains of a man who had made the ultimate sacrifice for them. His heart was touched, producing a flow of tears down his cheeks.

Sophia and Addison looked in several directions to try and guess which way the shomer had come from. They discussed numerous possibilities, and finally Addison said, "I don't think anything here will help us. We should return to Gabriel and see how he's doing."

Sophia thought for just a moment and asked, "Addison, if you were the fake shomer and had stolen the robe from Gabriel, where would you hide the robe?"

Addison's answer came quickly. "I'd destroy it. Burning it would work just fine, and my actions would earn me brownie points with the evil mastermind in charge of this job."

Sophia paused for just a moment, smiled at Addison, and said, "Then let's search the trash bins for burned remnants of clothing."

The two backtracked, rechecking trash bins and nooks and crevices where ash or traces of burned clothing might have been disposed of.

Finding nothing they decided to rejoin Gabriel. Just rounding the corner, they saw Gabriel sitting motionless on a bench, apparently deep in thought. Gabriel stood up as soon as they arrived and said, "I have the robe, and we must hurry because I received a message from Shamar. He said we should get to the Temple of Canopus as quickly as possible. Grabbing their hands Gabriel began to say a prayer when Addison interrupted.

"Stop!" I'll say the prayer, and all of us will just hold on to each other. None of us has time for any misadventures." Addison recited the prayer, and the three were transported.

The phantom and Senka entered the phantom's plush suite, and he offered Senka a seat on the couch. She sat immediately, having learned that all his requests were actually demands and anything short of immediate compliance led to pain.

She could never have imagined how many ways pain could be administered, but every day she accompanied the phantom, she discovered more. Tears formed, and she began to shake as she tried not to think about what was in store for her now.

The last twenty-four hours had been horrible for her. The phantom hadn't allowed her much sleep; last night he had been shocking her with fiery bolts of lightning and laughing as she screamed.

He took immense pleasure with each bolt that struck her, and she noticed that every time she shrieked, his power seemed to grow. Fear kept her from voicing her opinion.

But this time was different. He sat down in a large comfortable chair facing her and just stared. It was a long wait before he said anything. "You know, Senka, you are one of the most fortunate women here on earth. And soon you will be the most famous. You have been chosen by Lucifer to bear his child. Odd, isn't it, that you, of all women, would merit this honor?"

Crossing one leg over the other and tapping his fingers on the arms of the chair, the phantom continued. "I can't imagine why he picked you, but I don't question Lucifer; I just obey.

"I have been working on this project for a number of years, and no one can stop me.

"In spite of all your failures, and Vincent's as well, I shall be victorious for Lucifer. It's clear to me that the individuals trying to gather all the necessary artifacts for the ceremony are no match for dealing with someone like me.

"Nearly every one of them is unskilled at fighting; actually, their capability to fight against me is laughable. They think that they can defeat me, but I shall show them who the skilled warrior is. Even if they rally together, they are defenseless against me, and I can and will take care of them myself.

"So, Senka, it is time for me to take you to the ceremonial place to meet Lucifer, but first we shall get you appropriately dressed and then leave for the ceremony."

▲ ▲ ▲

They landed in the dark. After shaking off the chill from travelingAddison immediately said, "Just a moment, and please, no one move. I have flashlights in my backpack."

Sophia reached out and felt Gabriel's arm. She grabbed on to it and pulled herself closer to him. Gabriel put his arm around her waist and quietly said, "It's going to be all right, and as soon as we have light, we can make sure we are in the correct part of the tunnel."

It wasn't long before Addison turned on his flashlight, and then he handed lights to Sophia and Gabriel.

Addison and Gabriel flashed their lights around, looking around to ensure they were where they should be, but Sophia didn't turn on her flashlight. Instead she continued to cling to Gabriel.

Gabriel could feel her hand trembling. He looked at her and noticed tears in her eyes and saw a very frightened look on her face.

Gently he took her into his arms and asked, "What's wrong? We've arrived where we need to be, and I'm sure your parents and Shamar and Moses will be here soon."

Sophia placed her head on his shoulder and softly wept. Gabriel held her firmer in his arms and gently rocked her. He was at a loss as to what to say and decided that silence might be best.

Addison gave a small sigh and began shining his flashlight around on the ground and walls where they had landed. He sighed again and then asked, "Gabriel, I wish I could have told Sago good-bye, and I think that you should have allowed me that choice."

With Sophia still in his grasp, Gabriel quietly answered, "I was trying to spare you the memory of seeing Sago in such a dreadful condition. I wanted you to remember him as we all last saw him, a lost soul whose remorse about his past actions guided him to his final act on earth, which was to help his brother and friends escape their adversary."

There was a quiet moment, and Sophia spoke up. "I feel so bad over the way I judged Sago, and for what I thought about you, Addison. I now see that he did try to help me and that he helped all of us by showing us that our cell phones were bugged. I feel awful that I can never apologize to him and thank him for what he did."

Addison remained quiet for a while, then Gabriel and Sophia heard him clear his throat, followed by a voice that gently echoed with nervous tension as he stated, "Thank you."

Gabriel heard a noise, and with a take-charge tone of voice, he quickly and calmly alerted Addison and Sophia. "Sophia, get behind me."

Addison turned off the flashlight and moved swiftly to Gabriel's side. Gabriel added, "I think what I heard were someone's footsteps walking toward us."

The areas around them became absolutely quiet and remained pitch black. Each of them strained, listening for any sounds, but there were none. The hairs on Gabriel's neck, arms, and legs were standing on end as he became self-critical of their choice to be there. He anticipated that danger had somehow followed them and was approaching to slaughter them. An adjacent tunnel lit up from a moving light.

All of a sudden, a blinding light could be seen coming toward them. It was moving quickly and unswervingly. Gabriel prepared to strike the person now rushing toward them, and at the last second, he turned on his light to see his target. Just as the form reached them, Sophia and Addison heard, "Gabriel!" and "Shamar!" being shouted as they recognized who they were about to assault, followed by nervous laughter as they all felt relieved.

This was followed by Mariah calling out, "Sophia, I'm here." Sophia and Mariah embraced, and then Eli joined them in a family reunion.

Mariah quickly turned to everyone and said, "I'm thankful that you received the message and that we are all together again.

"Nonetheless, why did you leave the trailer? Moses told you to wait, and by leaving you scared us to death. And to make things worse, you increased the risk that you, actually all of us, could be captured.

"Now we aren't where we planned to be, and it could be dangerous to try and go where we should or want to be. We still have a lot to do, and I hope no one goes off on another excursion."

Eli spoke up firmly. "Mariah, we must discuss business. Our time is ticking away."

Mariah looked at Shamar and said, "Shamar, we must find a quiet secluded area in here to conduct some important business. We need an area where our voices won't be overheard if someone happens by."

With that, Shamar led them to a remote corner where it seemed that the acoustics would muffle their voices.

As they gathered, Addison began by updating Eli, Mariah, and Moses on all that had happened since they were last together. Mariah and Eli were distressed to find out that Sago was Addison's half-brother and even more shocked at the sacrifice Sago made for all of them.

There was a pause, and Eli summarized what the rabbi had written in his final letter and how it pertained to their recent activities. He went on. "I think, with the information in this letter and everything that Moses has added, we'll be able to pull off the ceremony."

"I agree," added Mariah. "To increase our chances of protection and success, we have an additional security option. If any of us stumbles into a grave situation where it is a matter of life or death, escape or capture, then you can robe back to Denver. Eli and I left the crystals in a post-office box for this very purpose. That choice is only for desperate situations, and if you must use it, we can keep in touch via the crystals on our robes.

"Now, Eli, Moses, and I need to travel by van to Jordan. Then the four of you will join us when we contact you that we have arrived safely at the appointed place for the ceremony.

"It's time to inventory our artifacts. Addison, please get all the flasks from your pack."

While Addison was going through his backpack, Mariah gave details to the group that the rabbi's letter clarified that the flasks added strength to each robe and then explained where each flask was to be placed for the ceremony.

Drawing a circle on the dirt floor, she pointed and said, "The stone of Aaron should be here at the center of a circle near the person wearing the robe of scrolls. Imagine the circle as being the face of a clock: The robe of scrolls is the center of the clock, and facing this person is the one wearing the phoenix robe. That person stands at noon on the clock. Those wearing the dragon and snake robes are at nine and three o'clock respectively.

"The flasks are placed in the appropriate positions and the wearer of the appropriate robe stands with his flask just in front of him or her.

"I think that Gabriel and Addison should be in charge of setting up the foundation of this ceremonial circle and place the flasks and Aaron's stone in the appropriate positions.

"Our robes will be worn or carried by the individuals assigned to them. This is what Moses, Eli, and I have decided, based on what the rabbi wrote, for each robe during the ceremony: Shamar, the dragon robe. Gabriel, you wear the snake robe. Moses, the phoenix robe, and Sophia, you will wear the robe of scrolls.

"Moses's robe will be carried by Eli to the ceremony. Sophia, you need to take possession of the robe of scrolls.

"These are the strengths of our combined robes: the yellow gems are for communication. You can listen in and hear what the person you are seeking is saying as well as send messages to that individual. Shamar and I used this method to communicate to you to get to the tunnels here at Canopus, and apparently it worked because here you are."

There was a surprise interruption by Addison. "Oh my, I forgot about this package that I have had for a very long time. It was given to me by Edward, and I have never opened it. But I think we should see what he so carefully wrapped for us and had me keep hidden. 'For the appropriate time,' I believe were his instructions."

Eli asked, "When did he give you this, and what did he say about it? Did he ask you to keep it secret, or did you do so out of loyalty?"

Addison thought for a moment and said, "I believe it was during his diggings in Alexandria. It may have been in or near the Great Library. I don't remember for sure. And I never opened it just in case you or another professor found it on an inventory list and requested it of me."

Eli placed his hand out for the package so that he could open it. Whatever he held in his hand didn't seem to be important because it was wrapped in ordinary brown paper. He felt the item under all the brown paper and realized it was surrounded with bubble wrap for protection.

Slowly removing the brown paper, Eli could see the bubble wrap, and just inside the wrap there were two items. As he carefully removed the wrap, everyone was shocked to see a beautiful stand that was made to support the accompanying vessel.

Eli held a phoenix flask that was magnificent in every artful detail that had been placed upon it. It was smaller than the other flasks, but the artwork seemed the same, but this flask was more exquisite.

They all stared in awe at the new flask.

Moses softly stated, "Eli, Aaron's stone should rest upon this stand and must be placed between me and Sophia for the ceremony."

There was a moment of silence, and then Mariah continued with the arrangement for the ceremony. "Shamar and Sophia need to carry the Scroll of Knowledge and the Scroll of Fate with them to our ceremonial location."

Without hesitation Moses spoke up with a small chuckle in his voice. "I'm certain you have not found a physical Scroll of Fate, is that correct?" Pausing for just a moment and receiving no answer, he continued. "The Scroll of Fate was concealed among the scrolls on the robe of scrolls, and that's why the robe of scrolls is so important."

Gabriel, in a low surprised voice, spoke up. "So that's why we had trouble finding it, and why he whispered to me not to worry about it, that we had it."

"Who whispered?" asked Addison. "Who whispered to you?"

"The man dressed like a shepherd," Gabriel quickly replied.

There were a few moments of awkward silence, and Eli asked, "What shepherd is he speaking of? Does anyone know?"

Addison responded, "I myself haven't seen or heard from a shepherd, but Gabriel told me a couple of times about such an individual. He said that when the mob was trying to burn him alive, the shepherd whispered the correct prayer to him. And when he dove into the water to retrieve the phoenix flask, he said the shepherd poked the hippo and shoved him toward the top of the lake. It seems that at those moments I failed to give his statements the attention they deserved."

Recognizing a similar event, Shamar spoke up. "That's right! I too recall when Theon also mentioned meeting a man dressed as a shepherd. It was when he first investigated the secret room in the library of Alexandria. He said that his initial meeting occurred after he read the disappearing scroll. And I think he met the same individual Gabriel is speaking of, an older man dressed as a shepherd. Theon also met this person on several other occasions but didn't say when or where the meetings took place, just that this individual always gave new or advanced clues about the gems and robes or assistance when a life was in immediate danger."

There was another quiet pause, and then Eli spoke up. "OK, it seems that we do have intermittent divine intervention helping to keep us on the right track."

"To continue on the setup," Mariah added, "the rabbi wrote that the Scroll of Knowledge should be placed between the snake flask and the person wearing the snake robe. And the Scroll of Fate should be placed between the dragon flask and the wearer of the dragon robe. This is where I am confused. Perhaps someone could help me out here; if the Scroll of Fate is on the scroll robe, how can we place it appropriately for the ceremony?"

Moses was quick to reply. "I begin the ceremony with a prayer, and I think that the prayer will release the Scroll of Fate to take its appropriate location."

Eli brought attention to himself by tapping on a box he had in his hand. "This box was given to me by the rabbi in ancient Alexandria to give to you, Moses. Is there something we need to know about this gift for the ceremony?"

Moses bowed several times and accepted the box. The wooden box seemed ordinary except for the ancient symbols and an inscription in an ancient Hebrew dialect that had been carved into the wood. It took Moses but a few moments to open the box. He checked the contents and then stated, "Yes, my friends, this is what I shall read to begin the formal ritual.

"It is a powerful scroll, and each of us participating in the ceremony will feel the full strength of our purpose, become aware of our allocated task during this rite, because of the power unleashed by this scroll to activate the divine force within each robe. We are now in possession of all that is necessary for this crucial mission."

Eli explained that he, Moses, and Mariah must go to the ceremony by way of Moses's van and that everyone else must robe in when they have arrived at the ceremonial site.

"Once we arrive, we will set everything up for the ceremony. The stone and flasks will be placed as Mariah instructed, forming a ring of knowledge, strength, and power.

"As we begin setting up, Mariah, Addison, and I are to keep watch and help; however, we must stay a short distance behind Moses. But none of the three of us will be able to enter the ring. That area belongs to Shamar, Gabriel, Sophia, and Moses. I don't know how we will be able to help, but I know we will recognize when that time arrives."

Moses stood and spoke quietly to the group. "We need to leave now. Addison, Shamar, Sophia, and Gabriel, it is important that each of you remain here, together, until Eli or Mariah contact you to come forward."

Mariah explained the reason. "I believe it will be safer and faster for all of us if just Eli, Moses, and I travel in the van since our itinerary includes crossing into Jordan and we have only our passports and Moses has his from the archeological department he represented here in Alexandria."

Mariah stopped speaking, and everyone could see sweat forming on her forehead as she placed her hand over her heart. All observed an obvious tightness in her chest. She slowly raised her other hand as if acknowledging that she was all right and ready to continue speaking.

Addison was trying to understand her body language, and he wondered if she was frustrated or uncertain. Perhaps her illness was progressing and she was trying to be brave. Either way, Addison was very concerned for her and how her illness might affect the rest of the team.

Watching others anxiously to ascertain how they reacted to the information, Mariah finally spoke in a low, somber voice. "I have a feeling that it is time for Eli, Moses, and me to head for the ceremonial area, which as you said, will be at the site of Sodom and Gomorrah, near the Dead Sea."

The sensation of being emotionally involved with everyone around him had affected Moses. His actions now would be the culmination of generations of preparation. And knowing for half his life that he had to be prepared to execute his responsibilities in the unlikely event that he would be called was no help when the situation finally came. Quickly he decided that he must take control of his emotions and face the enemy trying to make his decisions for him.

"Yes," he heard himself softly saying to everyone, "of course this was once a very evil place. Even today, evil's essence still lingers there. Eli, Mariah, and I will drive there and walk a very short distance from the vehicle to the ceremonial site. We'll keep in constant contact with you, and when we arrive at our destination, park the van and begin walking to our destination; this is when we will call upon the four of you to come join us. Eli will wear the phoenix, and it shall guide all of you to us.

"When we have reached this point, the location where pure evil will attempt to wrest control of all humankind, I am certain that all of us will be challenged by darkness, and this is when, by the grace of God, we will prevail."

The effect of his words could be seen in the looks on everyone's face. Moses had rekindled the confidence and aspiration to the group by reminding them of the importance of their success.

Gabriel mumbled, "Yeah, well, I agree and vote that Shamar, Sophia, Addison, and I wait here in the safety of this tunnel until we are called upon to leave. Those were really bad dudes who resided in Sodom and Gomorrah long ago, and if Lucifer wants to bring the values of Sodom and Gomorrah back, well I think we—Shamar, Addison, Sophia, and I—should begin planning on how to fight those evil forces."

Addison said he agreed, and Shamar and Sophia silently shook their heads in agreement as they clasped hands. Shamar thanked Moses for the pep talk and said it was just what they needed to hear.

Mariah and Eli walked to Sophia and said their good-byes. Then they wished everyone good luck. Mariah gave Sophia the backpack she had brought with her. She told her that it contained water and food for them to use during their wait.

Moses smiled, raised his arm, and waved good-bye to everyone. The three exited the tunnel to begin their trip to Jordan.

They listened until they could no longer hear footsteps, and then Gabriel, Addison, Shamar, and Sophia all huddled together and commenced making plans for how to spend the next fifteen to eighteen hours in this dark, damp tunnel while they awaited their summons.

They concentrated on what they could do to fight evil and its forces. Gabriel reminded them that they had the power within themselves to fight evil through their faith and strength in God and, for some of them, his son, Jesus Christ. Stillness came over the group as each listened to his or her own thoughts as to how to proceed.

▲ ▲ ▲

Starting the engine Moses said that he was very familiar with the southern route to Jordan. He explained that they would use the ferry at the Gulf of Aqaba, where they could cross. Mariah and Eli agreed, and Eli added, "That will perhaps give us an edge on anyone searching for us because it would save us from having to go through Israel."

Moses agreed, explaining that he had been concerned about going straight from Egypt through Israel to Jordan, which would be the quickest route, but with two Americans in tow who have no entry stamps on their passports, that would be harder than just going into Jordan from Egypt, which could still be problematic. He added that they needed to discuss this further, as he wasn't comfortable with their present arrangement.

Arriving at the Gulf of Aqaba, they showed their passports and bargained the price of the van and three adult passengers, round trip on a fast ferry. It was roughly $625 in American dollars. Moses choked a little when he heard the total price and gave the man his college credit card. It was declined, so Eli offered to pay for the trip with his personal credit card.

▲ ▲ ▲

The museum phone rang, and Karrie answered it. She was surprised by the caller on the other end. The fraud department of a credit card company was following up on the possibility of fraud in Aqaba, Egypt, with someone using Eli Daniels's credit card. The man continued, asking Karrie if Eli Daniels was in Egypt.

"No, I don't think so," Karrie blurted out, and instantly she felt that she had made a mistake in answering so quickly. *Perhaps,* she thought, *Eli has gone to Egypt. Could that be where he is hiding?*

"I really don't know," she heard herself saying as she tried to correct her earlier statement. "Eli Daniels has been gone for a week, and perhaps he did travel to Egypt. Give me just a moment and let me double check the schedule."

However, the person on the other end gave Karrie the direct eight-hundred number to the fraud department and a code-reference number, and then requested, "When you do see him again, please have him call us."

Distraught, Karrie hung up the phone. She had forgotten that she suspected the office phones were tapped.

Someone else hadn't forgotten though, and within minutes the phantom knew that Eli was at the Gulf of Aqaba and attempting to charge a fast ferry to Jordan.

▲ ▲ ▲

"What a disaster!" Eli exclaimed. "Now what do we do?" They all knew immediately that they had made a grave mistake by trying to use Eli's credit card. Moses, Eli, and Mariah returned to the van, and Moses contemplated their options.

"I can't drive two Americans without entry visas through Israel and into Jordan," Moses said. "We need another plan." As he spoke, he continued driving northward toward a port of entry into Israel, since there seemed to be no other way.

They continued moving toward Israel with no one speaking. Luckily the van afforded Mariah a place to lie down, and she took her medication and rested in the back. Glad that her condition didn't seem to be getting worse, Eli thought that she might be getting better.

Moses and Eli talked about alternatives for getting into Jordan. Moses suggested, "I think I need to leave the two of you here in Egypt, close to the Israeli-Egyptian border, and I could travel through Israel to Jordan alone. We need to get you a cell phone, add my cell number into it, and when I reach Jordan, I will call you and the two of you can use the robe to join me."

"That sounds like the most workable solution," Eli said. "Let me think about it. What worries me is the thought of me and Mariah just waiting for two and a half hours alone in a foreign town. Do you know of a place where you could leave us that would be safe?"

"Nuweiba" was Moses quick response. "It's large enough to get lost in, and it has a great bazaar and a few decent local restaurants, cafes, and shops. It is a big enough tourist area that you will blend in, especially with the clothing you are wearing. Also we can purchase the cell phone there. The two of you can have a relaxing meal, drink at the café, and walk along the beach if you want."

▲ ▲ ▲

Shamar, Sophia, Gabriel, and Addison were discussing all that they had been through the last few days, and they exchanged stories about all their recent experiences. Shamar shared his fears, hopes, and surprises at the amazing people and places and things that he had encountered. He said that he would miss Theon, Quintus, and Avitus and their men but was glad that they were able to help them and their families escape the violence.

Their conversations continued as they spoke of their expectations for this journey to end favorably. Suddenly the ground began shaking. It sounded as if the solid rock was splitting apart, and the skeletons that were stacked around them began falling from the walls.

"Grab your packs and run!" yelled Shamar. Everyone jumped up, grabbed their backpacks, and ran toward the entrance. Columns of dust were shooting up into the air, and rocks and dirt rained down on their heads as the skeletons continued cascading to the floor of the tunnel. The undulating floor of the cave made running difficult, and they were tripping as they grabbed for hand-holds in the wall that wouldn't stay still.

Addison fell, and Gabriel quickly pulled him back upright. Shamar and Sophia raced ahead of them. Reaching the entrance to the Temple of Canopus, Shamar realized that Addison and Gabriel were not as close behind them as he thought. He called out, and it seemed like a very long time until he heard their reply. Soon all four were fleeing from the entrance of the cave, out into the open grounds and kept running.

Once completely outside the cave, they heard people from the surrounding area screaming in fear. Gabriel asked, "Where are we going to go?"

Shamar answered, "We need to move away from this area, avoid the lake, trees and buildings, and find somewhere to wait. I don't—"

He was interrupted by a deep, loud rumbling sound. They turned toward the noise and beheld a large cloud of dust and debris being belched out of the entrance of the cave and rushing toward them.

Realizing the seriousness of their situation, they all began running again, this time toward the Citadel of Alexandria. They sprinted for several minutes and stopped when they saw the chaos and the damage before them. Boats were on their sides in the water, buildings showed some structural damage, cars had run into each other, and people were rushing around the area in sheer panic, uncertain of where to go and how to hide from the earthquake.

Gabriel said, "We have nowhere to go here, and our danger level just blew up in size. We need to robe back to Denver. We will still be able to robe to Eli, Mariah, and Moses when we're needed."

Addison's response was fast. He grabbed Sophia and Shamar by the waist and moved as close to Gabriel as possible and quickly said the traveling prayer.

Within moments the four were transported. They landed in a hallway lined on all sides by the open ends of mailboxes. Looking around they saw carts, piles of mail, and sorting equipment. "Follow me!" Gabriel yelled, and everyone rushed to an open door that led outside.

Loud and startled voices surrounded them as they ran: "Hey! What are you doing? Who are you? Stop!" But they ran faster, following Gabriel.

Once outside Gabriel said, "I know some people who have shops near here. We'll go there." They ducked around a corner, out of sight of the postal clerks, and picked up speed for a few minutes. Then they slowed to a fast walk in order to avoid suspicion. They finally arrived at a clothing shop, where Gabriel opened the door and ushered them in.

The man inside recognized Gabriel and, seeing the panting, sweating, desperate faces, realized that something was up. "We all need changes of clothes," Gabriel said.

"Are you guys in trouble?" his friend asked. "I'm not going to help with anything illegal."

"Nothing illegal," Gabriel responded. "We're being chased by some thugs. We just need clothes. We'll pay."

Skeptical, his friend sighed, and then agreed. It took a while for each of them to find suitable clothing, and when they were finished, Addison paid for everything.

They formed a huddle in a corner of the store and planned what to do. "We need to split up," Shamar said quietly. "The police might be looking for four people traveling together. I'll stroll with Sophia, and you two stay apart from each other but follow at a distance."

"Good idea," said Addison. "Let's go find a place to eat, and then we need to hide somewhere for several hours."

"Let's go to the movies," suggested Gabriel. It's dark, and we can stay there a long time while we wait for Mariah, Eli, or Moses to contact us.

Shamar and Sophia left first and headed to the predetermined restaurant. Gabriel and Addison gathered all the clothing they had been wearing, and Addison dropped off the clothes at a dry cleaner that was just around the corner.

Strolling to the restaurant as planned, they did their best to look innocent when police cars passed by.

Arriving at the restaurant, Addison and Gabriel met Shamar and Sophia. After eating, Addison opened up his backpack and distributed money for the movies. They again split up and headed to the movie theater.

With approximately ten hours to kill, they could see at least three movies and have another meal before they would need to robe back to Mariah, Eli, and Moses.

▲ ▲ ▲

Mariah awakened, and Eli told her of the discussion he and Moses had. "He's going to drop us off at Nuweiba and buy a cell phone, and then we'll enjoy several hours together while he travels through Israel into Jordan." He explained what Moses knew about Nuweiba and what would be available.

"I think it will be fun to stroll together on the beach," said Mariah.

▲ ▲ ▲

Tony was approached by one of his detectives and was shocked at what the detective said to him. It seemed that some people just appeared, out of nowhere, inside a post office in downtown Denver and then rushed out the door and departed into the streets.

What caught the detective's attention were the descriptions of three of the individuals. "These descriptions could apply to Addison, Sophia, and Gabriel, who until now had disappeared off the face of the earth. But of all places to show up, why a post office?"

Tony thanked his detective and asked for the security footage to be sent to him ASAP. Tony called Donald and explained to him what his detective had just told him.

Donald was a little surprised and quickly asked Tony, "You don't think they were looking for the map, do you? They could have thought we sent it through the mail. What's your opinion?"

"I ordered a copy of the security tapes from the post office," Tony told Donald. "You can watch them with me when they get here."

▲ ▲ ▲

Moses bought a cell phone for Eli, added his phone number, and filled his van with gas. At a small restaurant, he ordered some food for them. Leaving them at their table to begin the next phase of his journey, he reminded Eli and Mariah that he would text them as soon as he arrived at the appropriate spot.

"Thank you," Mariah said. "And this seems a really pleasant place for us to stay. I like Nuweiba, and I'm looking forward to walking on the beach with my sweetheart after we eat."

Moses left. After finishing her meal, Mariah decided to check in on Sophia. She had no problem following through with the procedure, but she was surprised by what she was hearing. Grabbing Eli's arm, she told him, "I hear explosions, loud cars, and gunfire. And the people are speaking in English. What's going on? Where are they?"

▲ ▲ ▲

Moses had just entered Israel when he saw several emergency vehicles with flashing lights rushing toward the boarder gate. Looking into the rearview mirror, he observed the guards shutting down the border gate between Egypt and Israel. His heart started racing, and he quickly turned on his radio. A bomb had gone off at a mosque. "This is not good," he said out loud.

He knew that this act would back up traffic and make crossing borders more difficult. He turned up the radio for updates and to help him assess the extended time this incident would add to his travel.

Soon travel became stop-and-go traffic. During one of the stops, he texted Eli and informed him of the situation and said that he would send regular updates to him. The good news, he texted to Eli, was that he was fortunate to have crossed into Israel.

▲ ▲ ▲

Shamar, Sophia, Gabriel, and Addison met at the food court of the movie theater. Sophia said that she was tired and really needed to sleep. Gabriel told them that in some of the theaters, there were larger seats at the back and that perhaps she and Shamar could seat themselves there and she could snuggle up and sleep in his arms.

Shamar liked the idea, and Addison just smiled. Addison reminded everyone to be sure and consume plenty of water.

It was time for each of them to return to the theater. Addison and Gabriel walked together down the aisle, choosing a seat three rows from the back, where Shamar and Sophia were moving toward the larger seat.

The movie was about to begin, and Shamar turned to face Sophia. Softly he whispered to her, "I love you and have something special that I wish to ask you." Pulling the box from his pocket, he opened it and proposed to Sophia. She was surprised but very happy. Taking the ring from the box, he placed it on her finger. Shamar then said, "Forever. I will love you forever."

Tears fell from Sophia's cheeks as she smiled and took him into her arms and kissed him. "Forever," she responded back to him. "Forever." Wanting to get a better look at the ring, she took his hand, stood up, and together they exited the theater into the hallway. She was in awe at the beautiful ring that he'd placed on her finger. She commented on its magnificence and uniqueness and the fantastic choice of the moon and stars and that each star had its own unique colored stone, which added to its one-of-a-kind beauty. She gave him a big hug and a kiss and said, "Yes, forever and ever." Slowly they both returned to the theater and the large chairs. Shamar took her into his arms and said, "Please try and get some sleep, or at least rest."

A few minutes after they returned to their seats, Addison and Gabriel moved from where they were to where Sophia and Shamar were seated. Addison smiled after seeing the ring on Sophia's hand. He congratulated them. Gabriel followed with his congratulations too. The four were seated close together, just waiting for notification from Mariah, Eli, or Moses.

▲ ▲ ▲

Just before reaching the border, Moses stopped and gassed up and took advantage of the break to buy food and some water. His next stop would be the border crossing that would allow him entrance into Jordan and bring him closer to the final destination.

The guard was polite and checked his passport and letter from the college verifying that he was a student on assignment. Within minutes he was on his way to the prearranged destination.

As he was approaching the designated area, Moses decided this would be a good time and place to pull over and try to speak with Eli. He was having a hard time getting a strong enough signal to speak, so he texted. Now he would enjoy his lunch and quench his thirst while he awaited a reply.

Moses looked out his front window and in a prayerful voice softly spoke. "Uncle Benjamin Katz, I wish you were here with me, and I want you to know that I like your friends and I believe you chose wisely. I was sorry to hear of your death and hope that you can guide me from heaven when I perform the ceremony. I barely remember what you tried to teach me; I'm sorry. But, please, if you can help me to remember, do so because I know I need your guidance. I shall miss you, your advice, and I know my mother will be very saddened when she is told of your passing. Rest in peace and know that I and your friends will do our best to complete your mission."

Just finishing his prayer to his uncle, Moses could hear the crunch of footsteps in the gravel; someone was approaching his van. Looking quickly out the side-view mirrors and then into the rearview mirror, he caught the vision of Eli and Mariah walking toward the van. He signed a big sigh of relief, waved at them, and smiled as they entered the doors to the van.

Eli said, "So far, so good, and we're thankful that you thought of this plan." Mariah sat in the back seat. She said that she had a relaxing time but was a little concerned that when she had tried to reach Sophia she heard gunfire, racing cars, and people communicating in English.

Moses thought for a moment and couldn't understand why she had heard such a thing. He said, "I purchased water for us, and I think that I should put on the phoenix robe, and that we should request the others to join us. I have driven to within ten, maybe fifteen minutes of where I think we need to be.

Eli stepped out of the van and gave Moses the phoenix robe. Moses immediately contacted Shamar and requested that they travel by robe to his robe.

It was a very short wait, and Shamar, Sophia, Gabriel, and Addison arrived just beside the van. Addison suggested that they each carry their flask for speed of setting up the ceremony circle, and then he handed the Scroll of Knowledge to Gabriel.

Eli suggested that he drive the rest of the way and that Mariah sit beside him. The others gathered in the back seats of the van, and Addison continued passing out all that was needed for the ceremony.

Fifteen

DESERT PYROTECHNICS

The phantom's bodyguard watched as the helicopter disappeared off to the west, leaving the three passengers alone in a barren section of a vast desert. After dusting himself off, he glanced over at his traveling companions, who looked entirely out of place.

The phantom appeared as an elegant-looking silver-haired gentleman in a tuxedo, standing beside a slender, beautiful woman, also in evening attire. Her dark, sparkling, velveteen gown, with a long slit up her leg and peek-a-boo cutaways teasingly placed around the torso, would have been quite at home at a Hollywood gala. To top it off, the woman had a black velvet collar around her neck, highlighting her smooth, ivory complexion. The collar was attached to a long silver chain that terminated in the gentleman's hand.

The guard looked around, noting the total absence of plant life. He had never seen such a desolate place. He wished the helicopter could have stayed, but the master didn't want any strangers to witness the arrival of the special guest. The large amount of money he had promised for picking them up would guarantee that the helicopter would return when they needed to leave.

"I don't see anyone around," the gentleman stated.

"No," the guard responded. "The past few days of minor earthquakes in this area have probably scared off any tourists, as well as the few archeologists who were nearby. I think we have the place to ourselves."

But even as he said that, a vehicle of some kind appeared in the distance, and it seemed to be headed in their direction. The three of them watched as it slowly grew from a tiny speck of reflected sunlight to an apparent car or van, winding its way in serpentine motions across the desert floor. Although it deviated off track as it made its way around hills and large boulders, it continued getting closer. It occasionally disappeared as it dipped into small valleys or got lost behind hills, but a small cloud of dust remained to verify that it was still coming.

"It's just a coincidence," the guard speculated. "Just a random traveler passing by."

"Coincidence?" the man snapped, betraying his annoyance. "At this place! And at this time? And someone just happens by? I've been around much too long to believe that this sudden visitor is here by chance."

"If he gets close to us, meet him and send him on his way." As if to voice its agreement, the ground shook for a few seconds.

"The ground is preparing for his arrival. We can't have uninvited guests around for the celebration."

▲ ▲ ▲

As Eli drove across the desert, following directions from Moses, he was looking around trying to spot anything that would depict a likely place to conduct a ceremony. The land was desolate, and he could see no unique features. *How does Moses know where we are?* Suddenly the van came to a complete and abrupt stop. Eli looked down at all the gages, trying to figure out what was going on. The van was dead.

There was a short pause, and Moses looked as if he was thinking or listening to something. In an instant Moses instructed Mariah and Eli to jump into the back seats. "Now!" he shouted.

Sophia, Shamar, and Addison moved as close as possible to Gabriel, while Eli and Mariah were moving from the front seat to the back. Moses, with the swift motion of his hand upon a seat handle, made his portion of the back seat lay down. He grabbed everyone as fast as he could, and they all formed a close tight circle with the phoenix robe encompassing all of them.

Moses nimbly scampered back over the backrest into the driver's seat, saying, "Be quiet, and don't move. A guard is approaching the van, and I can see a person dressed in a tuxedo and a woman dressed in a gown accompanying him."

The guard approached the driver's window. He scanned the inside of the van and slowly said, "You must leave. It's dangerous here."

The ground, seeming to agree, punctuated that statement with a brief tremor.

"I'm just a lone archeologist," Moses quickly and loudly responded to the guard, "and this place has historical value."

Hearing Moses's voice the silver-haired gentleman, who had been standing just behind the guard, also looked into the van to surmise its contents. He intervened, saying, "Let him stay. We'll make an exception in his case."

The man in the tuxedo paused briefly as if contemplating his next words to Moses, and then continued. "Let me guess; you must be the shomer. I think it would be fitting for the last person in a line of at least fifty generations of shomers to watch this event. If you survive this, you will be an ideal witness for the transformation of humankind into a perfect society, an event your ancestors have striven to prevent for centuries."

Hearing the old man's words caused heat to flush through Moses's body. He quickly opened the driver's door and left the vehicle. After a short walk away from the van, Moses stopped. In a deepening and shaking voice, Moses said, "Don't try to fool me about a perfect society. I know who you are and what you are doing. You are here to do the work of the devil. My advice to you is to stop now."

The gentleman laughed, and in a sinister voice, he snapped back at Moses, "You should bow down, for before you is the most honored of women. She is to bear Lucifer's child, and this child shall rule the world."

The old man jerked her chain, and she tried to speak, but only a squeak escaped her lips. The earth rumbled, and a wave passed under their feet as though they were on a ship.

"She's still trying to get used to the idea," the old man said. Turning to the woman he said, "Senka, it's time for us to prepare for the master's entrance." Senka squeaked again, still unable to talk.

Focusing on the end goal, Moses did not acknowledge his fear but chose to mask it. Again his voice rang with a bold, rebellious quality. "You say she is to be the most revered of women and you have an anti bark dog collar around her throat. This is how you treat humans? What kind of a world do you plan to have?"

Moses could see the anger on the old gentleman's face. He stood speechless for only a moment, and then he bent over and picked up a nearby chunk of stone, which immediately burst into flames in the palm of his hand. "Brimstone," he said. "I love how easy it is to ignite."

Closing his hand around the stone, he squeezed it until it formed a ball. He tossed the flaming stone under the van, and a fire erupted immediately, quickly engulfing the vehicle in flames. Yells and screams escaped from the flaming vehicle and quickly stopped. All that could be heard was the crackle of the fire as it devoured the van.

"Pity," remarked the old man. "And after all their hard work on such a difficult and mystifying task, they failed."

Moses stared at the flaming wreckage in horror, and his heart sank with this graphic evidence of his failure, as he watched the flaming tomb through the smoke and fire.

The guard was shocked and looked at the old man with a renewed fear.

"It is done. Back to the business at hand," said the old man as he turned and began walking away. The ground began rolling and shaking; however, its tremors were more violent, and the old man, the guard, and Senka had a difficult time staying on their feet.

Moses heard the old man say to Senka as they started walking away, "Now we wait for the master's arrival. Soon we will have one up on Jesus. We will have witnesses for your conception."

Moses glanced back at the van. The flames were gone, but the heat of the inferno distorted the air around the van, and scintillating waves in the air were proof of the extreme temperatures. The front bumper on the van took on the appearance of a smile, mocking his failure, as tears welled up in his eyes. Moses had a hard time fighting off the feeling of having been conquered.

After a few minutes, the ground lurched violently again, and Moses, trying to keep his balance, caught a sudden movement from the smoking van.

A touch of adrenaline raced through his body as Moses watched. Eli, Mariah, Sophia, Addison, Shamar, and Gabriel poured out of the van's burned doorframe. He quickly held his arms out wide as if to hug the world, and as the tears flowed, he thanked God in Yiddish for his friends' safe return.

The six of them all gathered together and began walking toward Moses, and Eli said, "A phoenix rises from the ashes, and thanks to you, we're back to complete the crusade."

As Moses embraced the group, his eyes sparkled with gladness. He was puzzled but glad they were alive and well.

Mariah was coughing and gasping for breath. It was apparent that the smoke and vapors from the fire were affecting her already weakened health. After a minute it became obvious to Eli and the others that she remained seriously ill.

Addison glanced at the van and then looked around his surroundings, fearing that the phantom might turn around. He quickly reminded everyone that they needed to move fast, as the earthquakes were getting stronger and that was not a good sign. Turning to Moses he asked him where they should form their circle.

Moses hesitated before speaking, as if gathering his wits or perhaps still skeptical of what he was seeing and hearing. Unexpectedly he lost control of his emotions, and his voice erupted with delight as he replied, "Right here where the van stopped. That is probably why it stopped, because we arrived where we are needed."

Gabriel handed Moses the phoenix robe, which had no damage done to it from the burning van, and then Shamar, Gabriel, and Sophia began placing themselves and their flasks where they thought their appropriate positions should be.

"I saw you, all of you, burn up!" exclaimed Moses. "Have you risen from the dead?"

"That was the phoenix robe," answered Eli. "It apparently transported us ahead into the time after the fire went out. So we weren't in the van when it burned."

Moses thought about that for a second and then busied himself with preparing for the ceremony. He put on his robe, looked to Shamar, Sophia, and Gabriel, reaffirming where he believed each should be, while wiping the tears from his eyes.

With renewed inner strength, he pulled the wooden box from the purple pouch, opened the box, and withdrew the scroll.

Addison, Mariah, and Eli slowly backed away from the circle, and Moses started reading the scroll. The ceremony had begun.

As Moses began reading the opening ceremonial prayer, one of the scrolls on Sophia's robe glowed with an opalescence and detached itself from the robe, appearing as a vapor that floated one by one to each of those within the circle. It paused over Sophia first, spreading fine, crystalline sparkles upon her. Sophia thought of it as pixie dust. Next it moved to Moses, then Gabriel, and then to Shamar. After each had been dusted with the radiance, they knew they had been touched by the spirit of the scroll.

After the scroll had blessed the four people in the circle with its holy dust, it drifted quickly to its preordained position within the ceremonial circle. The four of them immediately understood their instructions, which flowed as thoughts through their minds.

"The Scroll of Fate is the instrument from heaven that will influence your decisions so that you may save humankind from subjugation to evil. You must stay vigilant and on your guard at all times. You are protected from physical interference, but it is up to you to remain steadfast against verbal, or mental attacks. If you are diligent, you can defeat this evil and save the world. The fate of humanity is in your hands."

There was but a moment of silence, and then Moses turned his attention to Sophia's robe and began reading the appropriate scrolls as they each illuminated in the proper sequence.

There was a thunderous rumble as the ground shook again, this time with extreme force, causing fissures to open throughout the area. Parts of the ground and surrounding hills were set on fire by the earth's upheaval.

Mariah thought she heard a strange voice cursing at Moses with each word that he uttered. The tone of the voice frightened her.

Swiftly Mariah grabbed Eli's hand and then Addison's as she guided them further away from the circle. Addison became concerned and looked to her face to see if he could understand what she was doing. Was she seeking a place of safety for them to wait, or was she so frightened that she was panicking and really didn't know what she was doing?

Mariah stopped, and looking back and forth between Eli and Addison, she hurriedly told them that she heard a voice cursing at Moses as he began reading the second scroll and that this voice sounded as if he was trying to enter Moses's personal space to catch his attention and intimidate him into abandoning the reading.

She paused for a moment to catch her breath and then continued, saying that she understood the voice as saying, "Anyone who interferes with me will be punished" and, "They don't deserve to live."

Ignited by the spreading fires, glowing, spinning fireballs began rolling sporadically around the area in a dazzling display of natural fireworks. Some of the balls billowed smoke, and others spit fire, and occasionally some of the balls blew up, spewing flaming rock debris into the air.

Within moments Eli realized that he, Mariah, and Addison were becoming mesmerized by the light show as they stared uncontrollably at the numerous glowing balls that were rolling erratically around the area. Soon each ball's glow magically turned from a red glow to white, and then they all became undulating balls in continuous, swirling motion.

Understanding that it was hypnotic to watch, Eli warned Addison and Mariah of the danger. "Don't stare at the balls of fire; I believe they are part of a deliberate distraction."

Within moments the surrounding area was a large boiling cauldron of heat and turmoil. In spite of this, the fires and the movement from the earthquake did not seem to affect Shamar, Gabriel, Sophia, or Moses. A very faint outline of a dome could be seen encompassing them.

Moses's voice had grown in strength and clarity, and he exuded confidence. Everyone and everything within the circle changed.

The phantom had spun around as he heard Moses's voice reading the first scroll and then the second. He was shocked to see that those who had been in the burning van were alive. Admitting to himself that he made a mistake in assuming they were dead, he knew he had to focus on what remained in his control to make the necessary changes for his master's arrival.

"Wait here," he shouted at Senka and the guard as he rushed toward the small group of people, tossing bolts and flaming rocks, attempting to silence those who had formed a prayer circle.

The flaming rocks fell harmlessly to the earth, and the bolts he hurled immediately fizzled out.

Gabriel's and Shamar's robes radiated with an iridescent glow, and light beams streamed from their flasks, illuminating Sophia's robe, which had become too bright for anyone to look at.

Sophia herself appeared as an angelic figure with her head bowed and hands folded for prayer. Aaron's stone emitted a radiance that illuminated each person and flask within the circle.

As the heavens began to stir, the outline of a faint staircase could be seen forming from clouds and vapors. The bottom of the staircase had already formed down into the ceremonial area, and at the top in the sky, two tall angels in pure-white clothing descended confidently down it, exhibiting an atmosphere of saintliness.

Appearing at first to be apparitions, these angels assumed material form as they approached the ground and came into full view. Addison, Mariah, and Eli watched in awe as the angels positioned themselves at Moses's side.

Within moments three more angels, also in white robes, descended, and they each took their places beside Shamar, Gabriel, and Sophia.

Addison, Eli, and Mariah could no longer understand the words being spoken by Moses, and all three were overcome with wonder.

The phantom was surprised and frustrated at his inability to silence those in the circle, particularly because it was he himself who could no longer speak. His irrational reaction was to try again with different tones of his voice to yell the commands, and his continued attempts failed, as though he was wearing Senka's collar.

In his mounting frustration, the phantom turned to face those outside the protected area: Addison, Eli, and Mariah. The phantom forcefully grabbed Mariah, and with the touch of his hands on her arm, he inflicted painful burns. Mariah shrieked briefly and then resumed her coughing and choking, which were now mixed with piercing screams of pain.

Her screams temporarily distracted Sophia; however, it was just enough to cause a slight dip in the strength of the ceremony's protective walls. Although Mariah suffered extreme wounds, she managed to signal to Sophia to continue.

Through the agony of her wounds Mariah could still observe movements within the circle. A beautiful outline of a triangle was being formed between Shamar, Gabriel, and Moses, while consecutively a second triangle was being formed with Sophia at its center and the three angles positioned at each point of the triangle. Mariah whispered, "A Star of David." This new formation, along with Sophia, had become the center of the ceremony.

Sophia, struggling to overcome what she had witnessed happening to her mother, gently closed her eyes and concentrated on remaining steadfast so her robe could be read.

Tears streamed down her cheeks as she remained in her prayerful position. She wanted to help her mother, her father, and Addison but knew that this was exactly what the phantom wanted, a way to break into the ceremonial circle, disrupting the ceremony.

The phantom realized that he had found a strategy that could succeed. Although he couldn't touch those in the protected circle, Mariah's screams and choking affected Sophia, who had temporarily lost her ability to concentrate, bringing about a small rift in the protective circle. Even if he could break through for only a moment, it might be enough to interrupt the chanting by the shomer.

"A weakness," the phantom repeated to himself. With renewed confidence the phantom turned to Eli and grabbed him in the same manner, inflicting his arms with painful burns.

Mariah's choking overcame her, and she dropped to her knees as she struggled to breathe.

Sophia instantly heard the screams of her father, and she knew he was also writhing in agony. Her desire to dash out of the circle to protect them touched her soul, but she knew she couldn't; the only way she could help them was to stay focused and continue helping Moses with the ceremony.

The phantom realized that his actions had only caused Sophia's resolve to become stronger and that all within the circle could not only feel her determination to destroy this evil person but supported her endeavor to succeed.

The phantom watched as Eli staggered to Mariah. He gently took Mariah into his arms, cradling her head upon his chest and telling her how sorry he was and that he loved her. The phantom then waved his hands, and Eli was instantly healed, and his pain was gone.

Surprised, Eli looked up to the phantom, begging, "Thank you, thank you, but please heal Mariah too."

Making eye contact with Eli, the phantom said, "I can heal Mariah too, but I'm losing power, and it is your daughter's fault. I need you to stop the ceremony so I can concentrate on Mariah, on healing her, Eli, just as I have healed you.

"Stop the ceremony," the phantom repeated in a louder, more desperate voice, "and let me heal her, or you will live the rest of your life not only without your wife but also regretting that you couldn't prevent your daughter from causing her death."

Eli turned to look at Sophia and pleaded, "Please, Sophia, stop for just a few minutes so this man can save your mother." Bending down and kneeling next to Mariah, Eli lifted her torso slightly to show Sophia her dying mother.

Sophia did not look, but she had a vision in her mind in which she could see her mother dying. However, Sophia also saw that her mother was trying to communicate with her by silently moving her lips seeming to form the words, "No, don't. Don't do it, Sophia."

With forced restraint Gabriel spoke through his teeth to Eli, "No! Listen to me, Eli. What you are asking for would be a mistake. That man is lying. He's Lucifer's agent, and even if he heals her, he'll kill us all as soon as he has entered the circle and stopped the ceremony. Don't believe him."

Sophia's tears continued streaming down her cheeks, and she began sobbing aloud. Her arms felt heavy, so she clutched her hands together even tighter, sustaining her prayer position. She wanted desperately to assist her parents. Her angel looked at her and softly reminded her that she had free will and could leave or stay but that there were consequences for her choice, whichever way she chose.

With an emotion-choked voice but trying to sound calm, Shamar encouraged Sophia to focus on the ceremony, adding, "Sophia, your mother agreed to take the same risk as we all did, to give our lives to this effort, if it were to come to that. And she, even in her pain and suffering, continues to tell you not to listen to the phantom or your father. You should listen to her words and respect her choice, Sophia."

Sophia closed her eyes and pressed her hands together more firmly than before in prayer. She was praying for needed strength to fight evil and complete this quest.

Addison began to speak to Sophia, saying, "They're right," but these were the only words Addison was able to utter, because the phantom, furious with Addison, began striking him with lightning bolts that not only silenced him but caused him to collapsed into what appeared to be unconsciousness.

Not letting up and being utterly desperate, the phantom then snapped Addison awake, trying to persuade him to interfere with the ceremony. "You can stop this foolishness, Addison," he said. "You know I have power. Would you like to be a powerful man, Addison, not a servant? How would you like to have your brother back? He didn't have to die. Restoring his life will give you a chance to make amends, and in return you can rekindle the relationship you always wished you could have."

Inserting himself into the phantom's conversation, Gabriel shouted to Addison, "Don't listen! Sago sacrificed his life to stop this evil and save you and your friends. He would have died for nothing if you give in, and he won't forgive you, ever, if you choose the phantom's choice!"

Supporting Gabriel, Shamar forcefully spoke up. "Gabriel's right, Addison! If you stop the ceremony, especially by giving in to the phantom, then Sago would have died in vain. And he would be ashamed of you for your choice."

Throughout this turmoil Moses's voice continued, becoming stronger and more confident, and Sophia, who was highly alert to the situation, called upon her self-preservation skills to sustain herself.

The phantom's powers had withered, so he began pacing back and forth just outside the circle, and with both fists clenched and shaking wildly in the air, he screamed insults in a deep, thunderous voice to everyone within and without the circle, because this was all that he could now do.

Pausing in this tirade, the phantom then placed both hands firmly on his hips while planting his legs far apart, and yelled at Shamar, "Shut up, you fool! Don't you realize that your sweetheart will hate you forever because you are complicit in her mother's death and her father's guilt and misery?"

Yelling back louder, Shamar responded, "You are the murderer, and my sweetheart stands fast to protect humanity from your kind, even though she knows that you are willing to take her mother's life as a tool to trick her."

When he failed to help the phantom break the circle, Addison once again fell to the ground, paralyzed by the phantom or fear, and he watched and listened helplessly to all that was happening around him, sensing that his friends were paying the ultimate price, and that if he lived nothing would ever be the same. He would live the remainder of his life with remorse and with the memory of this moment.

Growing weaker as Moses's voice continued reading, the phantom, in anxious desperation, picked up another brimstone rock. But it failed to ignite, so in despair, he threw it at the group in the circle, where it fell short and dropped harmlessly to the ground. His strength ebbed, and he stumbled to his knees among the burning rocks.

The ground rumbled again, but weaker than before, and with the quaking everyone could hear what sounded like a voice conceding, "We are done."

As soon as the words were said, the phantom fell into an expanding crevasse, and while trying to climb back out, his clothes caught fire from the burning rocks.

An immediate feeling of relief passed over them, causing a release of all tension within their bodies and souls, and one and all knew that their battle had been won.

A man dressed like a biblical shepherd and carrying a staff could be seen descending the staircase. He arrived at the ceremonial circle and walked directly to the Stone of Aaron. Bending over he grasped the stone in his hands and placed it at the top of his staff.

The look on the phantom's face was one of shock and surprise. His understanding was that his power over this area, actually of the world, would be supreme because of his relationship with Lucifer. Making his way out of the hole, he pulled himself to his feet, glared at the shepherd, and began charging toward him.

The shepherd pointed his staff at the phantom, and within moments the phantom's body flew backward, but not before everyone heard a thunderous voice yelling, "No, no, I am to be their new god, their supreme ruler…" The voice grew fainter as it faded off in agony, and the phantom's body flew into the earth's open pit. The ground closed, and everyone remained silent.

Moses, exhausted, watched as the shepherd moved around the circle. The shepherd aimed his staff at Addison, Mariah, and Eli, and then stepped back a few steps, tapping the bottom of his staff on the ground.

Addison, Eli, and Mariah felt the strength from Aaron's staff penetrate every atom of their bodies. It was a sensation of healing and restoration. Each released joyful tears. Eli and Mariah hugged each other, and Addison looked first to Eli and Mariah and then to those in the circle. Tears flowed down his cheeks as he whispered thanks to God for his assistance.

Aaron turned to Shamar, Sophia, Gabriel, and Moses and bowed in thanks for their valiant efforts in defeating a powerful evil force and returning to God that which was taken many years ago. He then nodded in thanks to Addison, Eli, and Mariah, turning next to Shamar and Moses, telling them what remained to be done to complete their quest. He said a few words privately to Moses and the two embraced.

The last person to be spoken to was Sophia. As he approached her reverently, he noticed that she had tears running down her cheeks, and he could sense that she was honored to meet him but at the same time thankful that this ordeal had ended and that her prayer had been answered and her parents were saved.

Taking her hands into his, he spoke softly to her. No one else could hear this conversation, as it was conducted simply between Aaron and Sophia.

When he finished speaking to her, he turned to the group and said, "I am grateful for everything each of you contributed and your determination and steadfast loyalty to protect these religious relics, even when that price was dear to many of you. Moses and Shamar have been given the final instructions. I bid you farewell and thanks."

The angels gathered the flasks, and the shepherd returned to the staircase, which he began ascending. He was followed by all the angels, and just before disappearing into the clouds, Aaron turned to face the group and opened his arms wide. The heavens seemed to withdraw the staircase, angels, and Aaron himself back into heaven. They were gone in the glimmer of a second.

The surrounding landscape appeared as though nothing had happened, with the exception that Moses's van was no longer there.

There was a lingering silence as everyone slowly formed together while taking in all that had just transpired. Sophia gave her parents a hug; then she turned to Addison, Moses, and Gabriel for hugs; and next she went to Shamar and gave him a big kiss.

Shamar held Sophia in his arms for several moments, and when he began to break the embrace, she said, "Hold me just a moment more, please. When I am in your arms, I know that I am loved and protected, and right now I just want to hold onto that feeling."

Mariah waited for a while and then walked up to Sophia and commented on the beautiful engagement ring, and Eli concurred.

Moses spoke up, saying to everyone, "Addison, Aaron told me that Sago, who had given his life to defend those on this mission, had made peace with God before his death and wanted you to know that he is proud of you and grateful that his last effort was to help you."

Then he turned to Eli and Mariah and told them he also said that Edward and Patrick were both at peace and that Rabbi Katz was very proud of his friends for following through with his quest.

Moses stopped for a moment, as if searching for the appropriate words, and then said, "We have a few things to complete, and I suggest we get started now."

▲ ▲ ▲

Senka and the guard looked around where the battlefield had been, staring in disbelief at what had taken place before them. Senka's collar and chain had dropped to the ground, vanishing at the same time the phantom disappeared. Feeling free, she said to the man standing beside her, "I think you need to call that chopper to come pick us up."

▲ ▲ ▲

All seven of the adventurers gathered together. Moses said the prayer for travel, and soon they found themselves inside the Denver post office. An employee who remembered the memo on these individuals quickly slammed the exit door shut and locked it. He also alerted other employees, and one of them called the police.

It didn't take long for the police to arrive, and all seven of the adventurers were handcuffed and taken to the police station. When they entered the station, Mariah immediately requested Detective Tony De La Garza, since he was familiar with their case. The desk sergeant called Tony's office, and within minutes Tony and Donald appeared in the lobby.

Mariah moved quickly toward Tony and said they had a lot to tell him. Donald remarked out loud that he couldn't wait to hear what they all had to say.

Donald's attention was instantly captured by the four magnificent robes. He was interested in learning as much as possible about the gems and symbols on each robe and what they denoted.

At Tony's request, the handcuffs were removed, and everyone went to his office. Extra chairs were brought in, and all gathered around Tony's desk. Addison spoke up first and briefly brought them up to date on the events that had transpired from the rabbi's death to the present.

Tony and Donald asked questions during the details of the venture Addison was presenting, and naturally both men were in total disbelief, especially about the traveling with the robes.

Donald added, "I would love to have gone with you, if even half of this were true. What an adventure it would have been."

Shamar, understanding their skepticism, said, "OK, let me show you how these robes work. I will robe to the post office with you and Tony as my passengers, and we will retrieve the crystals that Mariah and Eli left in their post-office box, and then the three of us will all robe back here to this exact spot with them. What do you think? Want to give it a go?"

Donald and Tony looked at each other, and Tony, with skepticism in his voice, said, "Show me."

Donald was elated and curious but also doubtful, and so with a slower response, he finally smiled and added, "OK, let's give this experiment a whirl."

Moses smiled and said, "You are going to love this form of travel. Actually, it can be and is completely exhilarating."

Shamar put his arms around both their waists and said the prayer. Within moments they arrived where Shamar said they would, the Denver post office, and right beside Mariah and Eli's post-office box.

Donald was astounded, as was Tony. People within the post office were surprised to see people popping in again. Tony flashed his badge and quickly said, "It's OK, we are just here to collect evidence for this case. Go about your normal routine; we'll only be but a moment."

Shamar reached into Eli and Mariah's box and retrieved the crystals. He opened the box and showed the crystals to Tony and Donald. Donald was excited and asked, "These little crystals are beacons for traveling? Wow!"

Shamar said to Tony, "Yes. For traveling and communicating. All right, now let's get back to your office." Neither Tony nor Donald said a word. They put their arms around his waist and waited for the ride.

Arriving back at his office, Tony didn't know what to say. But Donald had a bazillion questions, and in his excitement stated that he wanted to learn more about these mysterious robes and crystals that served as a beacon for travelers.

Mariah turned to Sophia and stated that she was overjoyed at the impending marriage. Eli shook Shamar's hand and welcomed him to the family. He told Shamar that he thought the ring was the only one of its kind and that the moon and stars made her ring exceptional.

Tony looked around at the group, and said, "We don't have any justification to detain you any longer, and I can give everyone rides home. Where would everyone like to go?" He then added, "Gabriel, your car can't be released yet, so we'll give you a ride too."

Addison asked Tony if he could return to the mansion, and Tony said he could as soon as they completed the report and necessary paperwork. "Which won't be easy," he added, "since we will have to engage in some creative writing to keep the report believable."

Addison spoke, almost in a whisper. "Perhaps I could stay in the office apartment for a short while, since it's all paid for."

Gabriel asked if he could call his mother to let her know that he was all right. Donald directed him to a separate desk with a phone so that he could have some privacy. "Then I really want to go home," Gabriel added.

Shamar also added, "I'd like to call my family as well, and I need to go home too." Donald identified a phone for him.

"Could you drop me at my hotel?" Donald asked. "Bring Moses along, and we can get him a room so we can make our travel plans."

Moses said, "I have to get a flight back to Israel. Donald, perhaps you could go back with me and help me deliver the robes to the authorities. I can give you more details of our adventures on the flight."

"I'd be happy to do that," Donald replied. "And don't worry about it. I have special privileges for getting reclaimed antiquities and contraband through customs, and I know how to arrange to keep it with you, or rather, us."

Moses requested a special suitcase that he could keep the robes and crystals in, preferably something that could stay at his side, and asked Donald if he would help get his luggage past customs due to the antiquities value of the robes.

Excited, Donald added, "Can we stop in England first and show my co-workers the robes, before we go on to Israel?"

Moses made a pleasant facial expression and said yes.

"We just want to go home," Mariah stated.

But Eli interjected, "Yes, please, take them home, but I must stop at the museum. Drop me there, and I will get a ride home."

All of them walked with Donald and Tony to the police vehicle compound and entered a van. Tony dropped off Gabriel first, followed by Shamar, then Sophia and Mariah, Addison at the office apartment, and finally Eli at the museum.

Tony and Donald said good-byes to Eli, then Tony took Donald to his hotel. After they checked in, Tony suggested, "Since the flight doesn't leave until tomorrow, I would be pleased to have you both over to the house for dinner, and we can share stories."

Moses laughed and agreed to the evening plans.

Eli entered his office area and found Karrie busy at her desk. She looked up and saw Eli and ran to give him a hug and welcome him back to the museum.

Eli also participated in the embrace and said, "I have a lot that I would like to share with you; however, I think it should be done over dinner. Would you join Mariah, Sophia, and me for a long dinner engagement tonight?

We're closing up the office and heading to my home. Mariah will be glad to see you, and the three of us can share our experiences with you too."

Karrie said that she too had a lot to share with him and that she knew they would each have something fantastic to tell. "My story," she began, "is about men who oversaw the office while my boss was gone, and boy, oh boy, were they creepy."

The next day, Eli went back to work. Having missed the routine of the job, he activated the intercom. "Karrie, please contact Shamar. I need to find out how he's progressing on the Egyptian exhibit."

www.ingramcontent.com/pod-product-compliance
Lightning Source LLC
Chambersburg PA
CBHW050948120626
46552CB00001B/439